Books by Amanda Hamm

MORE LOVE IN ANDAUK
Evelyn's Granddaughter (#1)
Sarah's Friend (#2)
Eve's Brother (#3)
Simon's Mother (#4)

ROMANCE ARTS
The Art of Introductions (#1)
The Art of Patience (#2)
The Art of Communication (#3)
The Art of Friendship (#4)
The Art of Proposing (#4.5 ebook short stories)

LOVE IN ANDAUK
Everything Old (#1)
Into the Fire (#2)
By Its Cover (#3)
What Goes Around (#4)

They See a Family
The Study Group (ebook novella)

COFFEE AND DONUTS
Said and Unsaid (#1)
Sofie Waits (#2)
A Perfectly Good Man (#3)
Not Complicated (#4)

STORIES FROM HARTFORD
Andrew's Key (#1)
Jealousy & Yams (#2)
Collecting Zebras (#3)
The Christmas Project (#4)
Hearts on the Window (#0.5 ebook novella)

Beyond Wisherton (#1)
Back to Wisherton (#2)
Brelin and Wisherton (#3)
Baby of Wisherton (#4)
Birthdays and Wisherton (#5)

Simon's Mother

More Love in Andauk #4

Amanda Hamm

ISBN: 978-1-943598-25-0

 Before Someday Publishing

She wasn't going to cry over the loss of her job. At least, she wasn't going to cry in front of Mr. Tanner. The man had been talking about retiring since she started working for him. When he'd said that morning that it was time for him to retire, Tori had shrugged it off as another random comment about some elusive time in the future. She was struggling to process that he meant today. Today was the last day he was coming to work and therefore, the last day she would come to work.

He'd just asked her to read over a message he planned to record for anyone who called the office after it was closed for good. It listed the phone number of a company willing to take on new clients. Her eyes kept jumping to the words about his retirement being effective immediately, and everything else was slightly blurred by the tears she needed to keep unshed.

"Of course, I've already talked to everyone personally," Mr. Tanner said. "Been on the phone all morning. But just in case I forgot someone or someone forgets I called them, we'll leave that message up until the number is disconnected."

Tori nodded blankly. There was nothing to criticize in the message other than the fact that it put her out of work. Saying anything about that would only make Mr. Tanner feel guilty. Despite the shock of the moment, the man was 78 years old. He deserved to retire in peace.

"Don't stress about getting a new position for yourself. A talented girl like you will be snatched up quickly," he continued. "And you'll be paid through the end of the year so you don't even have to start looking right away."

Tori nodded more sincerely. "Thank you," she said. It was the day before Thanksgiving. There were still five or six weeks left in the year. Even in her current disappointment, she recognized that he was being extremely generous. The job she'd done the last three years only filled a fraction of the hours for which she was paid. He'd always been generous.

"You might start by calling Big Mike and Associates yourself," he said. "With the business I'm sending their way, they might be looking to expand their payroll."

"Yeah, um, I'll think about that." She handed him the paper with the message. "This sounds good to me."

"Great. I'll wait to record it until right before we leave. Otherwise, I'd likely turn it on by accident, and we'd spend the afternoon wondering why the phone wasn't ringing." Mr. Tanner chuckled as he spoke. He was aware his tech skills were lacking and never let it frustrate him. "You have a good lunch, and when you get back, I'll need you to help me pack up the office. My grandson is bringing a truck."

"Um... yeah... okay." Tori was trying not to sound shocked at how fast it was all happening. "I'll be back soon."

She grabbed her backpack from under her desk and slung it over one shoulder as she pushed open the front door. Most of the buildings on Main Street shared walls, but there was a narrow walkway between Mr. Tanner's office and Joseph's Gym next door. There was usually a pulsing beat from the gym. Joseph kept his classes moving. Tori must have left between songs as it was quiet when she started down the walkway, and she only began to hear a beat when she neared the back. There were a few parking places and a narrow gravel driveway. The stones crunched and slid under her boots. She crossed a quiet street and traipsed over more gravel in another alley before she cut through the backyard of the house. It was technically Tori's house, but she still had trouble not thinking of it as her mom's house.

She stood just inside the back door rubbing her hands together to warm up. It was extra nippy. She'd grab a hat and gloves for the return trip. It would be the last time she made that short walk. Her eyes burned again with that thought.

Tori set her backpack on top of her dryer. It was so close to the door, it had naturally become a shelf for whatever she was carrying when she came home. Then she squatted to let herself be welcomed and comforted by Fitz and Henry. The two tabbies circled her, alternately letting her pet them and mashing their faces against her legs.

"Hello, gentlemen," she said. "I'm happy to see you, too."

The quiet rumble of purring made her smile even more than the soft fur. After enjoying it for a minute, she checked the cats' food and water dishes, then opened the refrigerator to see what she wanted on her own dish.

Tori checked her phone while she ate. She frowned at a text from Simon. He was letting her know Fr. John had confirmed the meeting Monday night to discuss the Christmas Festival at the church. Simon was in charge of the planning for the festival, including securing enough volunteers. He continued to assume

Tori would be one of those volunteers. She would be happy to help and part of her liked that Simon knew he could count on her without having to ask. But another part of her was annoyed that he hadn't asked.

If she replied to this text, was she agreeing to an implied question about being a volunteer? That kind of felt like letting him off the hook. But maybe she'd already agreed by not refusing the several times the topic had been brought up. Maybe she was just cranky because Simon made her cranky. She replied, "Okay," and tried not to be annoyed.

Flipping to the Pans and Plates feed helped distract her. Simon's uncle and cousin, Dan and Noah, were the managers. Simon's sister Eve also worked at the pizza place and kept the social media entertaining with reports of her relatives' antics. Noah had convinced Dan to offer a special Christmas pizza and was rather obsessed with it, at least according to Eve. He'd been talking about Christmas so much that Dan had started banning related words from use in his restaurant.

Customers who followed Eve had taken to deliberately slipping those words into their orders to give Dan a hard time. There was a discussion about toppings that started with people saying they'd ask for merry mushrooms and use the alliteration to make it seem natural. One commenter insisted Dan had believed she said merry innocently. Tori knew he was way smarter than that, and laughed out loud at the idea. Some people seemed to think he paid no attention to the online chatter because he rarely contributed to it. He might be a day behind, but he always knew what people were saying about his pizza.

Tori laughed again when she found a comment asking if a good way to annoy Dan would be to order jolly jalapenos pronouncing the j as in English to get the alliteration. He was thoroughly roasted by a lot of the same people who said "merry meat, as in pepperoni" was unlikely to make Dan suspect he was being poked.

Eve's latest post, "Three different people told Dan he's a jolly good fellow today. I'm sure he doesn't think there's anything weird about that," had Tori in a better mood as she got up to return to work.

The office looked normal as she entered. Mr. Tanner had his door open so she could see him at his desk holding a phone to his ear with his shoulder. His hearing was not as sharp as his mind, which was why the volume was turned up so high Tori could hear bits of the other side of the conversation all the way at her desk. There was a budget sitting on it with a few sticky notes on how she should "pretty it up."

Tori set to work creating a prettier spreadsheet wondering if her boss had only been dreaming of retirement again. But she couldn't help overhearing the next phone call where he told someone he wasn't taking on new clients since it was in fact his last day before retirement. He said he was looking forward to spending more time with his wife, who was already making a list of places she wanted him to take her. The man on the other end seemed grateful for the recommendation of another financial planner and wished Mr. Tanner a happy retirement.

His office was quiet after he hung up except for clicks on his mouse and occasional creaks from his chair. Was he really about to give up the creaky chair and go home for good? Tori finished her spreadsheet and sent a notification to the man in the next room. She heard his computer chime though he probably didn't. He apparently saw it though because it was only a few moments later that he called out, "This looks great as usual."

A smile tugged on her lips, and she tried to keep it in place as the front door opened. There were no appointments that afternoon and walk-ins were rare. A young man entered wearing a baseball hat and a t-shirt with no coat despite it being less than 40 degrees outside. Tori wanted to ask how she could help and how he wasn't freezing at the same time she remembered Mr. Tanner saying his grandson was expected. The jumble of thoughts meant she didn't get any words out before Mr. Tanner's voice emerged from his office.

"Hey, Nick," he called. "Where are the boxes?"

"The, uh, boxes? Did you want me to bring those in right away?"

"Well, yeah." Mr. Tanner appeared in the doorway. "I don't have a lot to pack up, but I need to get started."

Nick nodded, glanced uncertainly at Tori, then retreated out the door without saying anything else.

"I don't know how he expected us to get everything in the boxes if they're in the truck."

Tori tried to think of a defense. "Maybe he wanted to be sure you weren't with a client before he showed up with moving supplies?"

"Clients know I'm done."

Tori shrugged. She couldn't think of anything else to say, though she wondered how many clients knew he was done before she did. Mr. Tanner had told her he was already semi-retired when he gave her the job. He'd said he planned to continue to pare down his client list and possibly close down the office within a year. He also assured her he was totally fine if she brought personal projects to work on whenever he didn't have enough to fill her time.

Since Tori had just finished college and still didn't know what kind of job she wanted, a light, short-term position had seemed a perfect filler while she figured out a plan for her life. At first, she'd used her free time to learn about possible careers. She'd taken some online personality quizzes and even set up a few appointments with Fr. John for spiritual direction. But life hadn't cooperated with showing her what she wanted. And Mr. Tanner said he was going to stick around "another month or two" so many times she got comfortable just letting the time pass.

Nick returned with a stack of cardboard under one arm and a roll of packing tape in the other hand.

"Give one of those to Tori and bring the rest in here," Mr. Tanner said before backing into his office.

His grandson – Tori guessed him to within a few years of her age – looked thoughtfully at the stack under his arm. He tucked his fingers under a flap and lifted his arm so that all but the one in his hand fell to the ground. He folded that box and set it on the ground to steady it while he taped the bottom. Then he held it out to Tori. "Where do you want this?"

She didn't want it anywhere. She didn't know what she was supposed to do with it. "I... uh... right here, I guess." She gestured to a spot on the floor next to her chair.

"I'm Nick Tanner, by the way. You're Tori?" He held the box near where she said but didn't drop it.

"Yeah. Tori Stillman."

"You're grandpa's assistant?"

"Yeah." At least, she was his assistant.

Nick nodded. He still didn't set the box down.

"How long does it take to tape a box?" Mr. Tanner called. "You'll have time to chat her up while we're packing."

Tori raised her eyebrows at the scolding. "He's impatient for a man who's been dragging his feet about retiring for three years."

"I guess he wants to get out before he changes his mind again." Nick smiled as he put the box at her side, a lingering smile that suggested he mistook her joke as flirting. Then he left Tori staring at the empty box.

The entire contents of her desk wouldn't even fill it halfway. She opened each of the drawers to confirm that. Pens, sticky notes, a stapler, a few empty folders and an ugly dinosaur paperweight left by the previous assistant went into the box. She found a roll of masking tape under the folders and another pen. It was all easy enough to move if Mr. Tanner had other plans for the box. The sound of tape stretching over other boxes came from the next room.

Tori took her box to the doorway. "Do you want anything other than what was in my desk in here?" she asked. "There's plenty of room."

"No. You can take that one home with you." Mr. Tanner was looking around the office instead of at her. "In fact, take some of this printer paper, too." He dropped a ream into her box, and she adjusted her grip to account for the extra weight.

"Um... okay." She didn't know if she'd have any use for the miscellaneous office supplies, but they might come in handy at some point.

Nick smiled at her. "He's got some interesting stuff in here. You might want to put that on your desk before he tries to give you anything else."

Mr. Tanner was eyeing a shelf of random gifts given to him by clients, some of which were uglier than the dinosaur. Tori returned to her desk and pulled a book out of her backpack.

She read slowly as she remained aware of the shifting and rummaging noises in the next room, and the conversation. Nick kept asking questions about what his grandpa wanted in each box and Mr. Tanner kept answering with things like, "Any box will do," "Wherever there's room," or "Your grandmother will sort it out later."

There were a few items Mr. Tanner instructed Nick to ask Tori about. The first was a blue vase. The flowers that arrived in it had been thrown out months ago.

"No, thanks," she said, hopefully loud enough for Mr. Tanner to hear. I already have a few vases and rarely have anything to put in them."

"That's too bad," Nick said. "Unless you don't like flowers?"

"Oh, I do. Some of them. It just... feels like a waste of money when they die so quickly."

"So, no one is buying them for you?" The inflection made it clear he was asking about a significant other.

Even though Tori was beyond sick and tired of having to tell people that she and Simon were only friends, she found herself wishing this guy believed they were more. It might save her from an awkward moment of turning him down. She simply shook her head and returned her eyes to her book to dissuade further questions.

Nick returned a bit later holding up a figurine of a guy hugging a glittery green dollar sign. It had been on the shelf since before Tori started. Nick widened his eyes to repeat Mr. Tanner's offer.

"I don't think so," Tori said. "I get that maybe someone thought the dollar sign might represent a financial planner, but it looks like an icon of greed to me."

Nick nodded at the figurine in what seemed like agreement. He said, "And I'm better looking than this guy anyway, right?" he turned it back towards Tori as he tipped his head in a pose that matched it.

Tori couldn't help but smile, though she tried to squelch it, then reopened her book. Mr. Tanner also offered her, through Nick, a wallet with a padlock larger than the wallet and an HDMI cable that he'd thought at some point would do something he couldn't get it to do. Tori suspected that no one actually thought she wanted those things but that Mr. Tanner was creating that opportunity to "chat her up" he'd mentioned. She did enjoy the banter about his grandpa trying to play an 8-track through the cable and where Nick might put the padlock to prank his sister.

The phone rang three times during the packing. Once it was a customer who'd thought of one last super important question for Mr. Tanner. Tori heard him giving the man his personal number. It seemed he still might not be 100% retired after the office was closed. Both of the other callers offered to lower the internet bill. She informed them the bill was about to be zero since it was about to be disconnected.

She had just hung up on the second telemarketer when Mr. Tanner appeared backwards through the door carrying one end of his desk. Tori jumped up. "Can I help?" Though he didn't seem to be struggling terribly, it didn't feel like a good idea for the retiring man to be carrying furniture.

"We got it," Nick said, just before he appeared at the other end.

"I can get the door at least." Tori rushed ahead to do that.

Both guys thanked her as they passed. She watched them, still holding the door, walk the desk about twenty feet down the sidewalk and set it next to a pickup truck. Both guys began to gesture, and she assumed they were formulating a plan to get the desk in the bed. It wasn't as massive as some desks, but it was pretty solid with three drawers on one side. Tori had a bad feeling that the plan was going to end with Mr. Tanner starting his retirement in the hospital. She was reasonably sure that was not on his wife's list of places to visit.

Her desk was the same. She was tempted to run into the office while no one was around to see if she could lift it. There was no point in her running over to help if she was only going to find out she couldn't get it off the ground. Tori glanced into the office, then at Nick opening the tailgate on the truck.

A white blur appeared that she quickly recognized as Joseph Zeibert emerging from his gym in a martial arts uniform. Joseph was a big guy that Tori guessed could put that desk in the truck all by himself. She breathed a sigh of relief and stepped inside to finally let the door close. Too antsy to take a seat, she paced the small area in front of her desk looking for anything else she could do. There was a clock on one wall, a landscape painting on the opposite wall and a fake plant in a pot by the door. The space was blander than Tori had ever considered. She grabbed the painting and set it on top of a full box in Mr. Tanner's office. His phone and computer were on the floor where his desk had been.

Tori returned to the front intending to do the same with what remained on her desk. Nick and Mr. Tanner met her from the outside at the same time. She asked if they wanted her desk next.

Mr. Tanner held up a finger to indicate he was thinking while his eyes scanned the area. They paused for several seconds on the clock, which made Tori look at it again, too. It was just before 3:30.

"This is it," he said with a definitive nod. "I'm going to record that message while you go ahead and unplug everything here." He went into his office and closed the door.

Tori leaned over her desk to shut down her computer before she unplugged it.

"The guy from the gym next door is going to help us get everything in the truck," Nick said, "which is good because I hadn't thought about Grandpa lifting stuff. He said there will be another guy when the class ends in a few minutes. Grandpa wants to get it all outside while we have help."

Tori nodded at the information. This really was it. She pushed down the lid of the laptop. It clicked into place as something inside her came loose. What was she going to do without this job? The only thing she knew was that she wanted to cry in front of this near stranger even less than in front of his grandfather. She mentally prayed for strength to finish the day. She unplugged the power strip and got on her knees to separate all the cables.

"Can I help?" Nick asked.

"I... um..." Tori stood up as she coiled the laptop cord to set it on top. "I think we need to wait for Mr. Tanner to get more instructions."

His office opened as she gestured to it. "Nick," he pointed at him, "pull out your phone and call my office to make sure you get the message I just recorded." He picked up the phone and began to wind the cord around it while Tori waited expectantly.

Mr. Tanner nodded towards the desk as his eyes met hers. "Go ahead and put that laptop in your box. You should keep that."

"Oh, I... can't accept that," Tori said. Leaving with pens and sticky notes was one thing. Leaving with a fairly expensive laptop didn't feel right.

"I insist," Mr. Tanner said. "I don't even know what to do with the one in there. I want you to find a use for this one."

Arguing when he sounded so sincere didn't feel right either. Tori slowly picked up the computer and said, "Thank you."

Nick was stuffing his phone in his pocket and gave a thumbs up.

"Great," Mr. Tanner said. "Take the tree out, then come back to help me with the other desk." He turned back to Tori. "I don't need you for anything else so you can go home now. But... please use me as a reference wherever you go next. I will have nothing but good things to say." He held out his hand to shake.

Tori accepted the handshake, but the departure still felt too sudden. "I can carry some boxes while you guys get the furniture."

"Nonsense." He waved off her offer. "That one box is enough for you to carry. Just carry it straight home."

"Okay. Um, thanks again for... letting me work here." She picked up the box and hoped he understood she was trying to say he'd been a great boss without being all mushy.

He smiled and said, "Happy Thanksgiving."

"Happy Thanksgiving to you, too." She moved to the door and pushed it open with her back. When she looked up for a final goodbye, Mr. Tanner had moved out of sight. Tori saw that Nick had already put the fake tree in the truck and was about to jump off the back. She quickly moved to the path between the buildings to avoid more small talk. She was not in the mood to be polite while holding a box of stuff that was now her former job.

Henry was purring on her lap, which helped a little. But he was also kneading enough that his claws occasionally poked her thigh. That was working against Tori's attempts at feeling thankful. She had told her mom she'd call before going to the Donnellys for lunch and was running out of time.

Her phone buzzed on the counter.

"Sorry, Henry." Tori pushed the cat to the side as gently as she could as she got out from under him.

The caller was who she expected. "Hi, Mom."

"Are you still at home?"

"Yeah. But I should leave soon."

"You were going to leave without calling me?" A gasp came through the phone. "Did you forget to be grateful for your dear sweet mother?"

"Yes. I think I forgot I even had a mother." Tori knew her mom was teasing and joked right back, which earned her a laugh before she continued. "Actually, I would have called you sooner, but Henry was in my lap, and you know he's cute."

"Ah, yeah. A snuggling kitty makes it hard to move. Just not as much as a snuggling baby."

"I know Ellie's at the top of your list this year," Tori said, "but I'm second, right?"

"I don't have the list in front of me right now to confirm that, but I think you're pretty high."

Tori smiled at the tone of feigned guilt. She tried to return to her chair, but Henry had sprawled across the entire seat. George was grooming himself on the one next to it. Tori walked to the loveseat to sit.

"How is your list?" her mom asked.

"I kind of shoved it aside to try again this evening."

"Oh, dear. What's going on?"

The Thanksgiving lists had been a tradition in Tori's family as long as she could remember. She even had vague memories of her dad making one. For a few years, Tori and her sister had gotten carried away with pages and pages of lists. In an effort to see who could make the longest list, they'd written specific foods and anything good that came to mind. Their mom had said they were losing the spirit of gratitude to the spirit of competition and could no longer add to their lists anything they could put in the same category as something else. That had shortened the lists, but it hadn't ended the competition. Eventually, they had challenged each other to list exactly 50 things, no more and no less. They continued to try to make a list of 50 each year since. Tori typically found it a great spiritual exercise.

"I started this year's list with the things Mr. Tanner gave me when he retired."

"What does that mean, he retired?" The air quotes on the word showed up in her inflection. Her mom had heard about his retirement enough to know he was never serious.

Until he was.

"He actually retired yesterday," Tori said. "He packed up his office and didn't even wait until 5 o'clock to send me home. I have no job."

"Wow. That's... sudden?" She sounded as though that might not be the right word for doing something after talking about it for three years.

"I knew it was coming, sort of," Tori said. "And I'm getting paid until the end of the year, so I'm not exactly panicking yet. I'm just... afraid of not knowing what comes next."

"You know you can always move to Florida."

"And you could always move back to Ohio."

She sighed through the phone. "It was easier when my girls lived in the same state."

"At least we get to hold it against David forever." David was Tori's brother-in-law. He'd taken a job in Florida shortly after he married Liz, something they both had felt was too good to pass up. Liz had gotten pregnant only weeks after the move and started hinting strongly that she'd love to have family around to help with the baby. Tori's mom was a teacher. She'd sent her resume to a Catholic school practically next door to Liz and David just to see what happened. What happened was she was immediately offered a job. She took it as a sign from the Holy Spirit that moving was the right choice. Being close to her first grandchild probably helped with the decision, too. Though Tori and her mom teased each other that it was David's fault they lived so far away, neither of them really held it against him.

"Have you told Simon about your job?"

"Not yet." Tori patted the space next to her when it looked like George was thinking about joining her. He jumped onto the other end and curled up just out of reach. She might have felt snubbed if it wasn't perfectly normal cat behavior. "I'd like to try to keep it to myself for today. I don't want to put a cloud over the Donnellys' Thanksgiving, make them worried about consoling me or anything."

"You could tell Simon and just ask him not to mention it to the rest of his family."

"I might have to if he's already seen the sign." Simon lived in an apartment above a store that wasn't directly across the street from Mr. Tanner's office, but it was close enough he'd pass it coming and going.

"And if he's already mentioned that sign to everyone before you get there?"

That was possible. "I think that means I should go now to deal with that. I'll send you my list tonight."

"Okay. I look forward to seeing you're in better spirits. Happy Thanksgiving, dear."

Tori had also received a text from her dad wishing her a happy Thanksgiving. She returned the sentiment before she stuffed her phone in her bag and went to the kitchen to open a can of turkey cat food. She spread it out on a plate so all three of her cats could eat from it at once. "Okay, gentlemen. Here's your holiday dinner." She set it down as she called to them. Henry was there before the plate touched the ground and the others close behind him. Then she put on her coat and pulled a salad from the fridge, her contribution to the people feast.

The Donnellys had a large garage with an extra wide driveway for additional parking. Tori recognized all the cars. The house itself was nearly as familiar as her own. Tori had spent a lot of time there since college, which was where she and Simon had become friends. When he'd started teaching at the music shop, she'd been there five days a week to give him a ride to work before he found a car he could afford. Simon had been the one to tell her Mr. Tanner was looking for a new assistant, and encouraged her to take the job even though it was temporary, saying it could at least give her a reference for whatever she landed on permanently.

She spent many weekends there since, mostly giving her opinions on the songs Simon wrote in his free time. Tori had spent a little less time in the house the last few months since Simon moved to his own place. But she still had a standing invitation for lunch after church on Sundays. She relished that time. With most of her family hundreds of miles away, she counted on Simon's family as a support system, even through sporadic awkward moments.

When they first came home from school, everyone thought they were being cagey about the true nature of their relationship when Tori and Simon insisted they were friends. The longer they went without announcing a wedding date, the more of his family seemed to get the message. But Tori suspected a few of them did not like the message, especially his sister Eve. Sometimes Eve looked at Tori as though she pitied her for not understanding how much she was missing by keeping Simon in the friend zone.

But Tori knew she was not missing out. Simon was easily the best friend she'd ever had. They got along wonderfully and talked about everything. He was always there when she needed him. She hated dismissing their relationship by telling people who had the wrong idea that they were *just* friends. Instead, she'd taken to telling people that there was "nothing romantic going on." She did wonder, however, if anyone interpreted that to mean they were dating and Simon was bad at it.

Sometimes she worried their relationship might not be sustainable if one or both of them started dating someone else. She almost never worried about that though because she almost never let herself think about it. And that brought her thoughts back to the job loss she also didn't want to think about and the fact that Simon might be telling his family about it.

Tori had parked on the street. She got out, grabbed her cold salad and hurried up the colder sidewalk. Simon's youngest brother, Matt, opened the door.

"Tori!" he said. "You can settle the debate."

She stepped inside. "There's a debate?"

"There's always a debate," Eve said dryly as she came up behind him. "I know Tori is practically family, but you should still practice your manners by taking her dish to put in the kitchen," she relieved Tori of the salad as she said it, "before you put her in the middle of whatever you and James are fighting about."

"Here, let me take that." Matt mimed taking a dish from Tori and then looked down at his empty hands. "Oh, wait, there's nothing here because my sister is super impatient." He shot the comment at Eve's back and rolled his eyes for Tori's benefit before he continued. "James thinks the Mary statue at St. Jude's has hair under the... uh... the cloth thingy that's over her head. What do you think?"

"Um..." Tori tried to bring a picture of the statue into her head. "I think the... uh, cloth thingy is far enough over her forehead that it covers all her hair, if I'm remembering right."

"No." Matt shook his head. "I mean, that's not the question. James thinks a wrinkle in the cloth, like by her elbow, is showing where the hair is under it, but the rest of us think it's just a wrinkle."

That was not a question Tori had ever considered before. "I don't think I can answer that without the statue in front of me," she said.

"I have a picture," James yelled from somewhere deeper in the house.

Matt motioned Tori to follow him to the voice.

James was at the kitchen table with a laptop open in front of him. Tori took her coat off as she walked and hung it and her backpack on a hook near the back door before she stepped behind James to see the picture.

"Look right here," he said. "See how the... uh, the cloth thingy... Does anybody know what that's called?"

His question went to the room at large, which had quite a bit of family scattered about. Simon was sitting on the couch with Grandpa Will and his aunt Michelle. Dan, Michelle's husband and owner of Pans and Plates, was chatting with Simon's older brother John near the opposite wall. An extra table was pushed against the end of the kitchen table to extend it into the living room. John's wife, Anna, was helping Simon's mother spread a very long tablecloth over the whole thing, towards James. Eve was coming down the stairs with a folding chair in each hand.

Eve said, "Veil?" while her mom said, "Scarf?" and Dan said, "Headdress?" They all sounded as though they were asking each other.

James shrugged. "I'm going to keep calling it the cloth. The cloth has this little extra fold right here that must be where the hair under it pushes it out."

Tori tried to look where he was pointing, but he had to pick up the computer to let the tablecloth pass under it. When he set it back down, she got a better view.

"Hey, Tori." Simon came over and lightly touched her lower back as a greeting.

She smiled that he looked happy to see her.

"That's not hair," Matt said. "It's just the way the cloth folds because her arm is bent below that. See?" He pointed to the same spot.

Both interpretations seemed reasonable.

"You should know," Simon said, "that when Matt told you the rest of us agreed with him, he meant the two people he could get to give an opinion."

Tori hadn't been concerned anyone would be offended by her answer, nor was she surprised by Simon's clarification of how many were even paying attention.

"Come on," James said. "It's hair, right?"

"Well, I could believe either," she said.

Matt made a scoffing noise. "Don't worry about hurting his feelings. I think he actually likes it when you call him a moron."

James reached back and jabbed two fingers into his brother's stomach.

"Ow! Mom!"

Mrs. Donnelly ignored him. He clearly expected that, and turned back to Tori. "Is it hair or a fold? The sculptor must have intended it to be one or the other."

"He's not here to ask," Tori said.

Simon nodded as though she'd said something wise.

"That's why I'm asking you," Matt said.

Tori studied the picture more seriously. Her hair fell in front of her shoulders as she leaned forward. She touched the end of her blond locks. "My hair falls straight down where on the statue, it'd be in front of the, uh, cloth. So I guess I'd have to say that's just a fold."

"Ha!" Matt gloated.

James closed the computer and picked it up. "It's a good thing I don't need anyone to agree with me to be right."

Tori smiled at the boys and momentarily wished she had younger siblings. Except she did have half-siblings so she knew she was really wishing for a more idyllic family. There was no point wishing for the impossible. She could hope to someday get married and raise a family more like the Donnellys than how she grew up. Except that might pull her away from Simon and the family she already loved. Tori forced herself to focus on the present.

Grandpa Will helped. He called out to Simon, "I thought you were bringing Tori over here to say hello."

"Sounds like a good idea." Simon touched her back again to steer her towards the couch.

Tori smiled at Grandpa Will as she got closer. He was of course not her grandpa. He had insisted she call him Grandpa Will when they first met. She hadn't known his last name at the time to call him Mr. anything, and he somehow wore Grandpa more like a title than a relationship. It quickly became a comfortable habit. "Happy Thanksgiving," she said. "What are you most thankful for this year, besides the obvious?"

"What do you call obvious?" He fixed her with a serious expression.

"Well... God, family, friends, uh... life." Tori had gotten at least that much on her list before she set it aside.

Grandpa Will nodded as though she passed his test. "Then I'm gonna say teeth."

"Teeth?" That was an answer she hadn't expected, which fit her stipulation.

He nodded. "My eyes have gotten pretty bad and my ears hardly work, but I have enough of my own teeth I still chew well. I'm going to appreciate that when all the food is before us."

"I'm definitely grateful for the food and the people making it for me," Simon said. "It hadn't occurred to me to be grateful I can eat it."

Grandpa Will tapped his temple. "You don't take even simple things for granted when you get to be my age." He was ninety-one. "Of course I brought my famous pumpkin pie. It's so creamy you could eat it without teeth."

"I'm looking forward to your pie," Tori said.

"You know how famous it is, right? It's on every can in the store." He chuckled at his joke.

Tori shared a smile with Simon over the familiarity of it.

"Noah's here!" Matt called from the front of the house. "Wait a minute. He brought a girl!"

The last statement caused more reaction than his arrival. Eve raced towards a window and several people began to murmur about who knew he was bringing someone. Someone said the name Sarah Franks.

On the one hand, Tori thought that was excellent news. It was no secret Noah had had his eye on Sarah for a long time. On the other hand, Sarah sold flowers out of the shop right under where Simon lived. She might have seen the sign if Simon hadn't. Tori mostly knew her through the young adult group at the church where they didn't talk one-on-one much. Sarah probably didn't know where Tori worked. Any change to the downtown in a town the size of Andauk was big news. Tori braced herself to assure everyone she was fine if it came up.

Eve opened the door for the couple after gawking at them through the window. The welcomes were genuine though effusive. Sarah blushed from all the attention. Noah grinned stupidly.

Sarah presented Mrs. Donnelly with several small bunches of flowers that were immediately spaced along the length of the table for decorations. Noah had also brought a sweet bread. Mrs. Donnelly took that to add to the buffet line as she announced it would open in five minutes. That was, apparently, the cue for the baby to start crying.

John and Anna had a two-year-old boy who had so far been content to fill a muffin pan with papers over and over on the floor. Tori presumed no one was going to be eating muffins that day. They also had a newborn girl who had been sleeping in a corner. Anna spoke softly to her as she picked her up, asking why she couldn't have slept just a few more minutes while her mom filled a plate. Tori took a few steps that direction in case Anna looked for someone to hold the baby for her.

Grandpa Will led a prayer before he was invited to be first in line for food. He made several comments about how no one was hungry if they wanted the slowest person to go first and how they'd all be very hungry by the time he was done fixing a plate. Simon walked behind him for assistance while getting his own food. Anna asked Tori if she'd mind holding the baby just until she got settled. They shared a smile over the polite wording of the request since they both knew Tori was eager.

She cradled the little one in her arms. The pink sleeper had tiny bunny faces on the feet. Everything about her was adorable, even the tuft of hair in the middle of a mostly bald head. Eve sidled up and peeked at the baby, who stared up serenely.

"Does she make you want one?" Eve asked.

"Someday."

"Me, too." Eve nodded at the shared sentiment, but her eyes flicked to Simon. She appeared to be trying to figure out if he noticed Tori holding a baby and if that gave him any ideas.

Tori felt unusually warm as she deliberately did not look at Simon. It was easy enough to pretend she wasn't doing that when the baby had her attention. While she was not in a hurry to give her up, the little one began to root and fuss about the time Anna returned with her plate. Tori passed her back to her mom. Only Mrs. Donnelly was in line behind her. The food was delicious and plentiful. Tori was able to get more in the spirit of the holiday as she listened to the happy chatter around the table. She didn't have a job, but she could still list 50 reasons to be thankful.

The local gym, not Joseph's Gym for families but the more traditional workout place, was open the day after Thanksgiving. It was quieter than usual, and Simon appreciated that. He listened to his own music so the literal noise level was the same. He didn't have to wait for any equipment though, and distractions were few. He took advantage of no one waiting on him to stay longer. His muscles were the good kind of sore when he went home for a shower. After a quick breakfast, Simon looked forward to several solid hours at the piano working on a new song. The song was barely an idea so far. He wanted strings that gave the impression of wind with lyrics about the Holy Spirit. It was vague, but he'd enjoy working to give it form.

Simon made the mistake of checking his phone before he started. There was a text from Grandpa Will that dented his mood. The message said, "Lpppking form and liggts tioni gght. Aat uno eying nee?" There were a ton of extra spaces that didn't clarify anything. Simon had no idea what he was being asked.

He loved his grandfather, respected him and was constantly entertained by stories from his long life. But it was so hard not to get frustrated by his communication failures. Grandpa Will's eyesight was poor, even with his glasses. He said that at the largest font, trying to read the screen was worse than the eye test where he tried not to blink while getting blasted with air. The comparison didn't make a lot of sense, but Simon understood the part about it being unpleasant for his eyes. He wanted to be sympathetic. The problem was that Grandpa Will used a magnifying glass to read the texts he received but couldn't be bothered to use it for what he sent. That seemed inconsiderate.

Simon stared at the message. By itself, he didn't have much hope of making sense of it. His grandpa had talked about wanting to watch the Christmas lights turn on though. With that knowledge, the words "lights tonight" appeared before the question. Grandpa Will could no longer drive, and Simon regularly gave him rides. It was reasonable to guess that he was asking about a ride, even though it had been established yesterday that Simon's mom was picking him up. Simon texted back, asking if he wanted Simon to pick him up and wording it to need a simple yes or no answer. Then he put the phone aside to work on his song. If Grandpa Will didn't have anyone around to tell him the phone had chimed, he might not respond for a few hours.

By the early afternoon, he had a few lines he liked, but he couldn't decide if it should be the chorus. He couldn't get a rhythm to the words. The shop downstairs was closed and beating on the bass drum sometimes helped. He stomped out several different beats. Nothing really sounded right. A walk might help. Simon went downstairs and walked up and down Main Street. He usually stopped in somewhere to exchange a few pleasantries. Light conversation put a song out of his head so that he could focus better when he returned to it. But none of his regular stops were open the day after Thanksgiving.

He did wave at Joseph and Emily Zeibert through the window of the gym. They were closed but hanging lights to turn on with the rest of the street. Tori had suggested that Simon should put up lights now that he was living on Main Street. He wasn't interested in hanging Christmas lights, but now he had mixed feelings about telling her that. If he had lights, she would have helped him. She probably would have made a nice display in his windows while he enjoyed the results. The trouble was that he was always on the verge of enjoying her company too much.

They had gotten to know each other in college. When he asked if she saw potential for them to be more than friends, she'd turned him down flat. The friendship had been shaky after that. Simon had tried to keep spending time with her so she wouldn't think he'd only been hanging around to convince her they should be together. That had absolutely been what he was doing, but he still didn't want her to think it.

Meanwhile, Tori had been rather nervous, probably worried that everything she said or did might be misconstrued as encouragement. But they had eventually settled into a true friendship. Or at least Tori had settled into a true friendship, and Simon had figured out how to pretend he was satisfied with that while he waited for her to change her mind.

The dynamic had been shifting since he moved out of his parents' house. A platonic relationship was natural when surrounded by other college friends or Simon's entire family. Now Tori occasionally visited him alone. The tension was untenable. He knew it was a matter of time before he crossed a line she didn't want or admitted how much he hated the boundaries. Either might mean the end of the relationship. That wouldn't make him any happier, and it would hurt Tori. All that meant he was constantly wanting to see her and avoid her at the same time. He returned to his apartment to think about wind and rhythm and not what Tori would think about any of it.

He picked up his phone as a message from Grandpa Will flashed on the screen. Prayer hands. Simon took it as a reminder to pray for patience with the old guy regardless of how he meant it. A minute later, he got another text with a clock and a winky face. Eve had been encouraging Grandpa Will to use pictures and emojis because she thought that might be easier for him than typing out words. It didn't seem to be helping his clarity. Simon guessed he was asking what time he'd be picked up. He replied with the time and tried again to do some work.

Simon's song started to come together until he recorded it with a ridiculous bassline. He erased that and realized he was not liking the chord progression. He shut off the keyboard and sat at the drum set to whack the bass more for stress relief than inspiration. A few minutes of classic rhythms later he was ready for some food. The Thanksgiving leftovers he brought home were as good as the first time.

Grandpa Will lived in an assisted living place only ten minutes outside of town. Simon finished dinner about fifteen minutes before he said he'd pick him up and grabbed his keys from the counter. He got a call from his mom before he made it to the door.

"Hi, Mom."

"Simon, are you going to the town lighting tonight?"

"I was actually on my way out the door to get Grandpa for it."

"You, uh... I'm on my way to pick him up." She sounded confused. "Didn't we say I'd give him a ride?"

"I thought so," Simon said, "but he was texting me today, and I guessed he was asking me for a ride."

"I suppose as long as someone gets him, he won't care who." There was a pause where she seemed to be deciding if she cared. "I'll go," she said definitively. "I called because I want you to save the bench in front of your place for us. Grandpa will need a place to sit, and I'd rather not tote chairs."

"Okay. I can do that."

"Great. See you soon."

Simon took a moment to parse the sudden change in plans. He looked out his front window and down the street to where the stage was set up. There were a few vendors under tents, and people were already milling about. He put on a coat and picked up a pillow from his couch before he went down. The stairwell was dim as it had no windows and one of the two bulbs had burned out. He'd been meaning to replace that before he had to navigate the stairs in total darkness. That other bulb probably wouldn't burn out tonight though. It could wait one more day.

Fortunately, no one had claimed the closest bench yet. Simon set the pillow next to him to have a good seat for Grandpa Will. He scanned some news headlines while he waited for everyone else. An interesting article made the time pass quickly.

Simon saw Tori first. She was walking towards him in the same black coat she'd worn since college. She had a bunch of different colored hats that she wore with it. The green one was pulled down over her ears. He liked the green one. He liked how beautiful her hair looked spilling out from under it. He liked that she wore it often because that was the one he'd given her. It was nice to know there was one present she didn't hate.

Tori's eyes were bouncing around as she took in the hot chocolate line and the people rushing towards the stage. They stayed steady when they landed on Simon. A big smile lit up her face and made his heart rate speed up. Simon stood up to greet her.

"Hi, Simon." Her smile shrank as she bit the side of her lower lip. "I guess you've seen the sign by now?"

"What sign?"

She seemed confused by his confusion. Then she pointed across the street. "The closed sign on Mr. Tanner's office."

Simon followed her finger. There was a closed sign in the window. It was the day after Thanksgiving though. Of course it was closed. Why was Tori looking at him like he was supposed to see something significant? "You didn't expect to work today, did you?"

"Not today." She sounded annoyed that she had to specify the day, but she was the one who seemed to think not working that day was somehow notable.

"What am I missing?" he asked.

Her expression showed disbelief. "You don't think it's a big deal that Mr. Tanner closed down his office?"

"I, uh..." Simon was at a loss for words. The grocery store was about the only place in town that didn't close for the holiday weekend. And it was after five so the office would be closed on any other Friday, too. It was clear that Tori was going to get upset with him if he pointed out any of that.

"I'm going to get a blanket," she said. She was already walking away.

"I can run upstairs faster than you can walk to your house."

"I'll be right back." Her tone was falsely cheerful.

Simon sat back down. Quite a few people were passing. Most seemed to want places closer to the stage. His family would be there any minute. Simon was concerned that Tori was postponing a conversation she didn't want to have in front of everyone. And it probably didn't have anything to do with vacation days.

"Eve!" He called to his sister as she passed by without seeing him.

She jumped and sent a guilty glance to Ben Shannon, who stopped next to her.

"Have you seen Mom or Grandpa Will?" he asked.

"No, but I just got here," Eve said. "We came straight from the church."

He wasn't surprised. Tori had come from the same group meeting.

"Are you meeting them here?" she asked.

"I think so." He explained a bit about Grandpa's texts throwing everyone off and how he was saving a seat.

Eve asked why Tori wasn't sitting with him.

Simon didn't want to say anything about not knowing what was up with Tori. "She went to get a blanket," he said.

Eve said, "Okay," and assured him she'd send Grandpa Will his way if she saw him. It was unlikely she'd see him first since she was walking away from the best parking. It was also fishy that she seemed to want to get away quickly.

Simon didn't have much time to think about her motives before he was distracted by family. His parents showed up with Grandpa Will and his two youngest brothers just before Tori got back. Matt brought a couple of friends. Simon gave up his seat on the bench to Tori so she could share her blanket with Grandpa

Will. Simon's cousin and his wife found them and stopped to chat when most of the lights were already off.

When someone on stage flipped a switch to turn on the tree, Christmas lights exploded up and down the street. Simon joined in as everyone sang *We Wish You a Merry Christmas*. He caught Tori's eye near the end. She smiled at him, and her expression said, "Thank you for being a good sport and singing this song you think is dumb." For those few seconds, it wasn't a bad song. That was more than could be said about the next song. There was a collective groan over the slow jazzy beat and the guy who hadn't mastered crooning. Grandpa Will announced he was done in, but the younger boys wanted to check out some lights up close and eat cookies. Simon's parents took Grandpa Will home intending to return later for the teens.

Simon was left alone with Tori. He joined her on the bench and tried to figure out how to invite her to talk about whatever she'd been nearly yelling at him about before.

Her eyes softened as he fumbled for something to say. "Apparently, you didn't realize the sign is new," she said. "Mr. Tanner put up the closed sign not because he's closed for the day, but because he's closed permanently."

"Whoa! He finally retired?"

She nodded somewhat sadly.

"What about your job?"

"I don't have one anymore."

"And he didn't give you any notice?" Simon thought Mr. Tanner was a good guy, but he suddenly didn't like him at all.

"No. But he's paying me through the end of the year so that's sort of notice."

Maybe Mr. Tanner was okay. "That's reasonable."

"Yeah. I don't know what I'm going to do, but he's given me time to figure it out."

"Is there anything I can do?" Simon asked. "Have you sent out resumes or tried to call anyone?"

"I didn't think there was much point trying to contact people over the holiday. "

"I guess you'll be doing that Monday then? I can spend the weekend trying to find some leads to send your way." He hadn't looked for a job in a few years, but he could search listings for something Tori might like. He tried to remember if he'd driven past any help wanted signs recently.

"Mr. Tanner said he put in a good word for me at the place that's taking over some of his clients," Tori said. "I'll probably call them first."

He was about to agree that was a good idea.

"But it's like twenty minutes outside of town," she said. "I won't be able to walk to work anymore."

"That's less than I have to drive, and it's not so bad."

She shrugged.

"Tori!" A woman on the sidewalk shrieked as though Tori was on fire. "I haven't seen you in ages." She swooped down to give Tori something probably intended as a hug. She patted both shoulders with a weird cheek bump before standing straight again.

"Hi, Abby. I hope you had a good Thanksgiving."

"Oh, I hate Thanksgiving," she said. "The turkey is the only thing I can eat." She pulled her coat open and ran her hands along her wide hips as though the motion explained why her diet was limited to poultry.

Once Tori said her name, Simon recognized her as someone from their high school class. "Hi, Abby," he said.

She gave him a half smile of acknowledgment before turning her full attention back to Tori. "You two must not be married yet because I don't remember getting an invitation to the wedding."

"No, we're not married and not getting married." Tori sounded exasperated. "There's nothing romantic going on here, just two townspeople watching other townspeople have stupid fun." She gestured to where a group of teenage boys – that included Simon's brothers – were doing the Macarena to the song *Chestnuts Roasting on an Open Fire*.

Simon hadn't noticed that. He paused a moment to enjoy the scene. When he brought his gaze closer, Abby was smiling at him.

"Not all ladies are as opposed to romantic happenings as Tori seems to be." Abby fluffed up the front of her hair while she tipped her head down to look at him through the fringe. It was likely intended as a flirtatious pose, but it looked as though she was trying to decide whether or not she needed a haircut.

"Uh, well, I hope you have someone to, uh... assist with those romantic happenings." He winced at his own wording. He didn't mind being direct, but that felt rude when she wasn't.

"I'm still looking," she said, then blinked a few times more than necessary.

Perhaps he hadn't been rude or direct. "I'm not," he said. "I'm happy with non-romantic happenings."

Abby blinked one more time, then broke into a huge smile as her eyes shifted back to Tori. "It was sooo good to see you. I hope it doesn't take long to run into you again." She leaned forward for another shoulder pat, this time whispering something in Tori's ear.

"Yeah, I'll see you around." Tori smiled politely until Abby's back was turned, then the smile dropped as she said, "If I ever do get married, she is not on the guest list."

"What did she say to you?" Simon asked.

"She said, 'He still thinks he's too good for everyone. Don't let him string you along.'"

Simon had nothing to say to that audacity.

But Tori let out a genuine laugh. "I hope you have someone to assist with those romantic happenings," she quoted.

"I'm glad you enjoyed that."

"Very smooth," she said. She shivered. "But I'm cold even with the blanket so I think I want to head home."

"I'll walk you," he said.

Ben Shannon appeared on the sidewalk, or rather, Simon noticed him on the sidewalk when he stood up. He pulled Simon aside while Tori folded the blanket to ask about Eve. He wondered if he should be concerned, but it turned out he was only uninformed. Simon set him straight and sent a quick text to Eve to do the same.

As he and Tori began to cross the street, Simon reached for her hand. To cover, he offered to carry the blanket.

"Thank you," she said, handing it over. Then she set a brisk pace to get inside where it was warm.

Tori had always sat on Mary's side at St. Jude's simply because that's where she always sat. The Donnellys had always sat on Joseph's side. As long as she and Simon were attending Mass with their respective families, no one gave it much thought. When Tori's mom left for Florida, it was Grandpa Will who insisted she shouldn't be left alone. He brought Simon, who drove him every Sunday, to the other side the first week and informed her that, "This old dog can learn new tricks when it means rescuing a damsel in distress."

All the Donnellys joked with Tori afterwards about all the "distress" she would have suffered and how Grandpa Will and Simon probably had trouble keeping up with the vastly altered perspective. But the three of them had sat together in the second pew of Mary's side - because he'd sat in the second pew of Joseph's side and a body could only adapt so much - nearly every week since. And despite all the jokes, Tori loved the company.

She arrived first and enjoyed the quiet of the nearly empty church before she heard Grandpa Will's voice in the back informing Simon, and the others scattered throughout, that she was already there. The pew creaked as he sat next to her, letting out a relieved breath. It made her a little sad to think that the walk from the parking lot had exhausted him. But she smiled brightly and whispered, "You're late."

He frowned with a twinkle in his eye and pointed at Simon. "It's his fault."

They both liked to arrive early and had developed a running joke of accusing whoever was later of being late. And if it was Tori who was first, Grandpa Will would always blame Simon. She met Simon's eye to share a smile of greeting with him before she returned to her book of gospel reflections and both guys pulled out rosaries.

As they walked out after the Mass, Tori knew what Simon was going to comment on before he opened his mouth.

"You're lucky you brought the readings with you because some of us weren't entirely sure Elijah wasn't talking to himself."

"I've heard people pronounce both of the those names a few different ways, but they usually try to emphasize some difference when they show up in the same passage." Tori tapped her missal. "Since I could see them, I think there was a subtle difference."

"Very subtle," Simon said.

Grandpa Will had asked them before to leave him out of any conversation until they got outside because it was too hard to distinguish their voices from others with so much of the congregation talking at once. A few people greeted him though, and he managed to make out basic pleasantries.

Tori walked with them towards Simon's car. When it was quieter, Simon asked Grandpa Will how he thought Elisha should be pronounced.

"Are you saying it wrong?"

"I'm asking you if I'm saying it wrong."

"Which prophet are you referring to?" Grandpa Will asked. "The one with a j has a long i, and the one with the sh has a short i."

"Um... is that the only difference?" Simon asked. "I would think j and sh sound different, too." Grandpa Will shrugged. There was a good chance he'd forgotten the first reading, and they'd made it to the car.

"I'll see you both soon," Tori said as Simon opened the door for his grandfather. She hurried to her own. Even though Tori had chosen not to share the news of her job loss at Thanksgiving, she found when she got home that day she was disappointed no one had mentioned it. Now she was looking forward to some supportive comments, just not how many times she was going to hear that she should have said something sooner.

She saw Simon helping his grandfather out of the car as she parked on the street. Moving a bit faster, she got to the back door at the same time to go in with family.

James met them inside and immediately raised his eyebrows at Tori. "Mom is gonna lower her glasses at you."

"Uh, oh," Tori said, though she wasn't worried. Mrs. Donnelly had a habit of pushing her glasses down her nose to look over them when she had something important to say. There was something oddly intimidating about it. She usually only used the technique when recruiting volunteers for church activities.

Mrs. Donnelly rushed up. "Tori, honey, the boys saw Mr. Tanner had closed his office after we left the town lighting. When did you find out it was closing?"

"Wednesday," she said. "He said it'd be the last day, but I didn't really believe it until we started boxing up the place."

"You were here all day Thursday and didn't tell us? Or Friday either?"

While her glasses stayed in place, James stood behind her with his low on his nose. He nodded along with a stern expression that made it difficult for Tori to keep a straight face.

"I didn't want to spoil the holiday for anyone," she said.

Mrs. Donnelly shook her head. "You are too thoughtful."

James wagged a finger.

His mom elbowed him, though she was also trying not to smile. "What you need," she said, "is a hug." She wrapped her arms around Tori.

Tori sank into the hug and squeezed back. She did need a hug and hadn't realized it. "Thank you."

Once she let go, Simon's mom said, "I know you'll land on your feet. Come, help me get lunch on the table."

She'd known Mrs. Donnelly for years as the scary lady who talked people into doing stuff at church before she knew her as Simon's mom. The two personas were occasionally difficult to reconcile. Tori followed her to the kitchen. Eve was pulling a pan of something that smelled like cinnamon out of the oven.

"There's a pan of strawberries on the stove," Mrs. Donnelly instructed. "Find a spoon for that and set it on the table."

It felt good to know which drawer to open for a serving spoon and which one held a trivet for the pan. The familiarity gave Tori a sense of belonging. She set the pan on the table, near where Simon and Grandpa Will were taking seats.

"Oh, I'll take a big piece," Simon said, evidently guessing what was coming next.

"I'll see what I can do," she said.

Eve was cutting and putting pieces on plates to bring to the table. Once everyone had a serving, they said a prayer together before passing around the warm strawberries.

"What are we having?" Grandpa Will asked, looking at his plate.

"French toast casserole."

His eyes scrunched. "Why did you mangle it?"

"It's French toast *casserole*," Mrs. Donnelly repeated.

"But *why* is it mangled into a casserole?" He sounded genuinely confused.

"When I do it this way, it can bake while we're at church." James snorted as he tried to stifle a laugh while his mom explained. "Otherwise, I'd be standing over there dishing out a few slices at a time."

Grandpa Will either accepted the reasoning or forgot his question while he was helping himself to strawberries. He said, "You know what this reminds me of? The time James made us grilled cheese sandwiches."

"Oh, dear." James hung his head.

"*Those* were mangled," Simon muttered.

"The boy thought he could improve on the conventional wisdom for grilled cheese." Grandpa Will smiled at the memory.

"I was like, eleven," James said.

"Rather than cutting the sandwiches in half after they were finished," he continued, "James tried to cook them on one slice and fold them in half. Toasted bread didn't want to fold, I guess."

"I reversed the ratio so there were two slices of cheese on each slice of bread, and that part was actually genius because *cheese*."

Matt nodded at the assessment.

Tori agreed there was merit to adding extra cheese, but she'd heard the story before. She knew the end result did not reflect genius.

"First he tried to push one corner over to the other and couldn't get them to line up."

"At least one he pushed right off the pan," Mrs. Donnelly supplied helpfully.

"Then I think he tried to fold them over the spatula?" Grandpa Will eyed James expectantly.

"I held a butter knife along the diagonal and used the spatula to fold some very nice triangles."

"Until you pulled the knife out and all the cheese came with it," Eve said.

"Not all the cheese," James said. "And weren't you supposed to be supervising me? Did you not know melted cheese sticks to everything?"

Eve chewed her bite of food quickly for a comeback. "There's only so much you can supervise someone who refuses to listen. And I think I did stop you from trying to fold them with your hands so at least one of us knows that melted cheese is hot."

"That was quite the platter of misshapen sandwiches set before us that day."

"Everything stuck together and did sort of resemble a grilled cheese casserole," Simon said. His expression was a mix of surprise and amusement. "Which means I actually see the connection."

Tori smiled at him. She understood his surprise since Grandpa Will regularly started his stories with "this reminds me of" when he meant "this is something completely unrelated that just popped into my head."

"What are you going to do with your vacation, Tori?" Matt had just returned to the table with a second helping. "And pass the strawberries, please."

She picked up the pan, but Simon's dad said something before she could.

"An unexpected job loss is not a vacation."

"Unexpected?" James laughed.

Matt also sounded disbelieving. "Dad, none of us, least of all Tori, is surprised Mr. Tanner retired."

She smiled at their protest. She knew she'd sat at that very table speculating that the retirement would happen within the month at least half a dozen times. She had always assumed he would tell her a retirement date two or three weeks in advance, and she would not get paid after that. Even though she ended up being surprised by the way it happened, she couldn't honestly call it a bad surprise. "I will have some unexpected free time," Tori said. "I'm thinking about doing some more thorough cleaning around the house than I have in a while."

"That's not how you take a vacation," James said.

"It's not a vacation." Mr. Donnelly softened his expression before he turned to Tori. "I'm sorry the boys are being insensitive."

"They're not. It's really..." She wanted to assure everyone that it wasn't a big deal. But if that was true, why had she been afraid it would dampen the holiday mood? She decided to change the subject. "At least I'll have more time to help with the Christmas Festival." Tori sent Simon a pointed look.

He only stared blankly a few moments before he picked up her hint. "Yeah. We're meeting with Fr. John tomorrow to make sure everything is coming together."

Mrs. Donnelly nodded gratefully and refrained from asking any follow-up questions.

This was Simon's first year heading the festival committee, which he'd taken over at his mom's request. He'd been annoyed that she wanted him to handle it but didn't seem to trust him to handle it. Tori suggested that if he made an effort to communicate his thoughts and progress on it, she'd ask him fewer questions.

"You said to remind you to let me DJ," Matt said.

"Right. We'll get you on the official list tomorrow," Simon said.

Matt nodded and grinned wickedly at his mother. "I know exactly which song to play first."

"Don't you dare," she said.

He was only teasing and seemed pleased with the reaction. "I think I'll actually start with *Baby Shark*."

James rolled his eyes. "That's not a Christmas song."

"You're not officially the DJ yet," Simon warned.

"This reminds me of mowing the lawn." Grandpa Will jabbed his fork towards Eve, who might have been the only one who hadn't said anything, let alone anything that could have reminded him of something. "Or not mowing the lawn maybe, like the time Michelle didn't mow the lawn."

Tori noticed several knowing smiles around the table. The fact that no one else looked confused meant she was probably the only one who hadn't heard this story before.

Grandpa Will apparently picked up on her interest because he focused on her as he began his story. "Dan and Michelle had only been married a few months when they got into a little tiff over the lawn. This was before he opened Pans and Plates. He was working long hours to save up for it over at that restaurant near, uh... Was it Tiffen or Swanton?"

It appeared he was talking to himself, but Tori shrugged to confirm that she couldn't help. Pans and Plates had been open longer than she could remember. She only knew those two cities weren't particularly close to Andauk, or each other.

"Catawba," Mr. Donnelly said.

Grandpa Will didn't hear him.

"Catawba," James yelled.

"It'll come to me later," Grandpa Will said, "but it's not really the important part of the story. Because of the long hours, he had let the lawn get taller than he should have. Michelle decided to mow it for him. She pulled the mower out to the front yard, but she couldn't get the thing started."

"It's funny when she tells it," Matt interjected. "She says she put all her weight into pulling the cord, but her hand slipped off and she tumbled into what she describes as the world's most inelegant cartwheel."

"Poor girl just wasn't strong enough. Of course, this was before they made mowers that can start just by pushing a button. I bet even someone as old as me could get one of the newfangled ones going. But back when... After she couldn't get it started, she left it in the yard thinking she'd try again when her arm was less tired. But Dan came home first. He thought she put it in the yard as a not-so-subtle hint that it was time for him to get to work on that yard. He took care of it before he even came in the house, then came in dog-tired and cranky."

Tori winced. The story sounded more like a set-up for an ugly misunderstanding than a laugh.

"Don't worry, honey. He didn't yell at her or anything." Grandpa Will's eyes sparkled with delight at telling the story to someone who didn't already know what was going to happen, though even those who did know were following his animation closely. "Dan kept quiet to keep the peace. Unfortunately, Michelle could tell he was testy and thought he was upset with her for failing to mow the lawn. She was embarrassed about not being able to do it so she didn't say anything either. And then a few weeks later, the lawn got overly tall again, and I think I will take one more small slice of that mangled French toast. It's pretty good."

Simon jumped up to get it for him.

"Thank you, John."

When Grandpa Will accidentally called Simon his older brother's name, a chorus of voices corrected him before he corrected himself. "I left you all with tall grass, didn't I?"

Tori nodded.

Matt said, "You left Dan and Michelle with tall grass."

"Right." Grandpa Will winked at him. "Dan started to get worried that she was getting angry with him for taking so long and would leave the passive aggressive hint in the front yard again, probably on a day he was particularly beat. And Michelle thought he was intentionally leaving it for her to do because he was still mad about having to do it the last time. Dan came home one day, took a look at the lawn and knew there was no way she wasn't already boiling mad. He planned to face it instead of letting her get angrier. He walked inside and blurted, 'I'm too tired to mow it tonight,' which caused Michelle to burst into tears."

Matt and James snickered, not so much at their aunt crying but at the way Grandpa Will relayed it as a wholly unexpected turn of events.

"Dan had prepared himself for yelling. He didn't know what to do with tears." Grandpa Will shook his head in sympathy. "He said he dug deep for the energy to go back out and cut the grass."

"He just left Michelle crying?" Tori asked.

Simon leaned forward - he was sitting directly across from Tori - and said, "He thought doing what she wanted was the quickest way to get her to stop. Have I really never told you this story before?"

"No," she said simply, ignoring the intimacy behind his surprise that there was anything he hadn't told her. Simon had mowed Tori's yard for her all last summer. That was a likely time for the story to have come up. Perhaps they had too many other things to talk about.

"They finally talked and got everything straightened out afterwards," Mrs. Donnelly said.

"That's the funniest part when Dan tells the story." James cleared his throat and lowered his voice slightly in an attempt to sound like his uncle. "Important life lesson, boys, mowing the lawn is never the answer."

There was a ripple of amusement around the table, though it appeared Grandpa Will had lost interest and was slumping in his chair.

"Are you ready to go home?" Simon asked him.

"If you're ready to take me. Otherwise, I can try to find a more comfortable chair for a nap."

Simon stood up. "I'll get our coats."

He took Grandpa Will home while Tori helped clean up lunch. She stayed for a quick game. She would have stayed longer if Simon had returned. But she knew he wanted to work on a song. Mr. Donnelly offered to walk her out, which was something he'd never done before. She was therefore not surprised that he had something to say, though she was surprised by what it was.

"Tori." He stopped her on the back porch. "I know you're smart and capable and will find work soon, but if there's anything we can do financially... we just want you to know we'd rather you come to us than let stress over a gap in income make you take a job you'll hate."

"Uh..." Tori was momentarily speechless at the offer. "Thank you. I... I hope it doesn't come to that, but thank you."

He nodded. "You're far from alone. God has your back, too."

She smiled at the reminder and moved down the steps as they exchanged waves.

Simon gave the bass three firm whacks, this time in satisfaction. The song was starting to come together. Unfortunately, he needed to set it aside if he was going to have time to stop at his parents' house on the way to church.

He had doubts that it was a necessary stop. His mom had texted the request because she had something that needed to be returned to the church office. With all her volunteer work, his mom was in and out of the church nearly every day. It was difficult to imagine something so urgent it needed to be dropped off after hours when the only people who would be there were the few on the Christmas Festival committee. Simon suspected she had some input about the festival, and that was what she really wanted delivered. But when your mom asked you to do something, even if you're an adult, it was generally in your best interest to do it.

There was a WWII-themed board game on the kitchen table when he came through the back door. It appeared it had been set up but not started. He was trying to determine which scenario was on the board when his mom approached.

"The boys have homework, but they got the game ready as an incentive to work faster or something."

He nodded at the explanation as his eyes continued to assess possible strategies from his side of the board.

"Thanks for stopping by," she said. "I'm kind of embarrassed to have walked off with this stapler today."

Simon looked up to see his mom holding out a black stapler for him to take. "A stapler? That's what needs to go to the church immediately?"

"Yeah. I was shuffling a lot of papers today and somehow ended up with that in my bag."

It wasn't the first time his mom had accidentally brought home something that belonged to the church so it was a plausible excuse. Sort of. "And you can't just bring it back tomorrow?"

"I'm not expected until afternoon. Someone could need to staple something in the morning."

"And St. Jude's only has one stapler?"

"I've never counted the staplers. Have you?"

She was determined to keep up her cover, and he did only have a few minutes. "Fine," he said. "I'll take it back for you. Is there anything else I can do while I'm here?"

"Well, since you asked, I did think of the perfect gift for you to get Tori for Christmas."

"Really? What?" He'd mentioned he was struggling and would rather get something Tori liked than something he thought of on his own.

She pushed her glasses down and met his eyes far more intently than a present idea warranted. After a pause, she said, "An engagement ring."

Simon couldn't laugh when he was being stared at with a this-is-not-a-joke expression. Not that he thought it was funny. He wanted to laugh so his mom would know she'd said something so far-fetched it made people laugh. "I can't do that. She'd think I'd gone off the deep end if I tried to propose out of the blue."

"No, she'd think you finally came to your senses."

He stared at his mom for a long minute, trying to figure out which of her senses made her think she was suggesting something rational. Could she possibly have a legitimate reason for thinking Tori would be receptive to... No. Tori hated it when people assumed there was more to their relationship. She would not appreciate this attempt at interference.

"The two of you are obviously a match made in heaven," she said. "I don't know how you got stuck in this just friends rut, but one of you needs to move out of it. As the man, moves are traditionally your domain." Her words remained firm. She pushed her glasses up as she finished though, and her expression transformed from stern to near pity.

That was more than he could take. "Thank you for the stapler, Mom. I'll see you later." He retreated out the back door.

The drive to the church was not nearly long enough to get the conversation with his mom out of his head. Fr. John was at the door to greet him, and to let him in since the office was locked in the evenings. Two more people were expected so the priest stayed at his post while Simon continued to the conference room around the corner, dropping the stapler on the reception desk on his way. Tori had evidently arrived just ahead of him. She was still hanging a coat on the back of her chair. She stuffed a blue hat in its pocket. At the sight of her, Simon couldn't help imagining her gladly slipping his ring on her finger. A bright smile lit her face. It was as beautiful as ever, but knowing she had no idea what was in his head made it painful at the same time.

"Hi, Simon. You're late."

"That only works on Grandpa Will," he said. "There's still five minutes before the meeting starts. Mrs. Collins, right?" He turned to greet an older woman seated at the table. She was probably 60ish with small but deep creases by her eyes. Simon recognized her because of the size of the church but had never been specifically introduced.

"Yes. You can call me Debra though."

"Simon Donnelly," he supplied and was not surprised when she nodded as though she already knew that, too.

Fr. John came in with two other women, Mrs. McGrady and Mrs. Larson, and took a minute to make sure everyone knew everyone as they took seats. Fr. John had only been assigned as the pastor of St. Jude's since the summer, which made him the least familiar with the event they were about to discuss. He opened with a short prayer, then sat back to let Simon take over.

"Thank you, Father." Simon pulled up some notes on his phone. "Mrs. McGrady, I think you said you wanted to handle the food? How's that going?"

"Wonderful," she said. "Pans and Plates will provide the pizza at half price so that'll make it easy to stay in budget. I already have most of the ingredients for the cookie decorating station, and Noah Farwin even offered to bake half of them for me."

"Do you have enough people to serve and run the booths?"

"I think so."

"Great." Simon made a note that the food was covered with a reminder to check in one more time. "Travis Shannon, who couldn't be here tonight, is handling most of the games. I already talked to him. But he needs volunteers for the tree undecorating, and I thought maybe that's what you could do, Tori."

She considered that. "The church already has the tree and ornaments from last year, right?"

"Yeah. And we ordered St. Jude's ornaments for everyone who participates. You only need to find some sort of prize for the winner and probably at least one person to help you reset it."

"I'll ask Eve," she said.

His sister would almost certainly cooperate and enjoy it.

Volunteers from the sixth-grade class traditionally performed some comedy at the festival. Simon turned to Mrs. Larson to ask about that.

"Those kids are going to be the death of me," she said.

Simon braced himself to hear about the first hiccup in the planning.

"I had to veto the first two ideas," she continued. "The first was simply the kids standing around a tree saying things in baby talk. I had to tell them it wasn't funny, and they weren't hard to convince. I think it was a silly idea most of them had already tired of. But then..." She shook her head, mashing her lips against a smile. "One of them apparently heard the story that St. Nicholas allegedly punched Arius at the Council of Nicaea. And they used that to write a whole skit called 'Santa punching heretics.'"

Simon felt his eyes widen. He noticed Fr. John scratch his nose in an attempt to cover a smile.

"Most of the kids lined up in front of the one playing Santa and said increasingly ridiculous things, and then waited for him to... He pulled his fist back and sometimes got a running start and... They wanted to do sound effects and bring in a mat so they could fall over after the fake punches and..." She paused as she fought another laugh.

“Were these actual heresies?” Simon asked. He didn’t think it mattered if the play had already been vetoed, but he couldn’t help his curiosity.

“The first two did say, ‘Jesus was just a man,’ and ‘There are three gods,’ but then they were just saying things like ‘Eggnog is gross’ or ‘this or that is the best Christmas movie.’”

Simon nodded and glanced around. Tori kept a straight face, but he recognized the laugh in her eyes. Debra Collins looked less amused.

“I admit I laughed so hard I had tears in my eyes,” Mrs. Larson continued, “mostly because of how much fun the kids were having. But I still had to tell them to try again. You know someone will get upset if we have kids fake-punching each other. It’s a bad example for the younger attendees, plus, well... Santa.”

Simon nodded at the biggest problem. “The first thing my mom said when she handed me the reins was ‘Don’t let anyone talk you into involving Santa.’”

“The kids are workshopping something with a white elephant party now. I think the third time will be the charm.”

“Okay. I’ll get in touch with you later in the week to see how that’s coming.” He looked at his list again. Raffle prizes. That was what Debra Collins had volunteered to cover.

“I’ve had a good response from several of the local businesses, most of whom donated something last year,” she started. “But just about everything is some sort of, uh, gift card or service. I’m hoping to get something more visible to attract attention day of. I went to that new place, the Floral Creations place and was informed that they *sell* items. They don’t give them away. I tried to explain that everyone at the church would see it, and it’d actually be fairly cost-effective advertising. She said I was welcome to have something for *our little raffle* if we paid for it." The disgruntled expression she ended on confirmed she did not end up with a floral creation, whatever that was.

"Have you talked to Sarah Franks?" Tori asked.

"Who?"

"Of Franks' Flowers. I bet she'd donate something beautiful."

"Sarah provides the altar flowers every Sunday," Fr. John added.

Appreciation lit Debra's eyes at this information, and she picked up her phone from the table, presumably to make a note about talking to Sarah.

They talked about when and where the raffle tickets would be sold before the festival and during, then moved on to a few other topics. The decorations were going to need the most future discussion because Simon cut that off when it seemed in danger of getting heated. Cleanup needed a few more bodies. Other than that, Simon felt the event was promising. He told everyone he'd gotten through his list and no one had any questions.

Debra Collins said she had to run. Mrs. Larson wished everyone a blessed evening as she followed her out. Mrs. McGrady asked Fr. John about altar server training. Her husband helped with that ministry and wanted to get a new training session on the schedule. They stepped outside the conference room as they talked.

Simon was waiting for Tori. She had her coat buttoned and her hat pulled over her ears. The way her eyes followed the others suggested she was waiting for them to leave.

"I've been thinking about the undecorating prize," she said. "My first thought was some really tacky tree topper with lots of flashing lights because I thought people who didn't like it would at least think it was funny." She stepped closer and lowered her voice. "But, uh... the reaction to tinsel is making me rethink that idea."

Simon nodded. "It might be safer to stick with... I was about to say a more traditional topper, but..." He thought back to one lady insisting white lights were boring while another insisted colorful lights were trash. "I'm not entirely sure what's safe."

She bumped his arm. "Way to give me the hard job."

"I... might be able to find something."

"You *almost* sound sincere." Tori laughed at him. "I know how much you hate shopping. Maybe I'll find something while I'm looking for a present for you."

While he was grateful she wasn't going to accept his sincere but very reluctant offer, he was less thrilled by the reminder of their ongoing argument. He thought they should agree not to exchange gifts. She insisted they didn't have to agree on anything. She was going to give him a Christmas present whether he got her anything or not and that letting her do that could be his gift to her. They would need to continue outside though as it sounded as though Mrs. McGrady was leaving and Fr. John was probably ready to lock up and go home.

Tori slung her backpack onto her shoulder and they both turned to the door. The priest was not in a hurry to leave after all. He put a hand up to ask them to wait.

"I wonder if one or both of you might give me a minute to explain, uh... I seem to be the only one who doesn't know why Santa is a taboo subject for this festival. I've been hesitant to ask for fear of putting my foot in my mouth or stirring up... But I'm dying to know the history."

Simon glanced at Tori to see if she wanted to explain.

She made a motion of deferring to him. "Everything I know comes from Simon anyway."

"Everything I know comes from my mom," he said, "but I've been hearing about it pretty much my whole life so I know it well." He started at the beginning. "St. Jude's has been doing the Christmas Festival for at least thirty years. It used to be in early December though, instead of right after Christmas. My mom has been on the committee or running it since the beginning. Until this year, of course. She says every year for like fifteen years they had the exact same argument about Santa. There was a group who insisted there had to be a Santa, that all the kids would be disappointed if there was no Santa. And there was another group that didn't want Santa because they thought he represented the secular/consumerist side of Christmas that no church should encourage."

Fr. John nodded grimly. Perhaps he'd heard a similar argument at a previous church. Or he just knew how sides could become entrenched.

"Some years they had a Santa and some they didn't, though my mom says that had more to do with whether or not someone volunteered to play the role than who had the better argument. Every year at least one family refused to come and let everyone know Santa was the reason, either his presence or absence. A lot of people hated that what was supposed to be a fun community-building event always left someone with hurt feelings.

"This one year, and I sort of remember this but only vaguely – I think I was nine or ten so not old enough to care about church politics – there was this older guy who came up with a compromise that actually worked. Rather than set up a place for kids to come sit on his lap, parents were told to help the kids with letters ahead of time. He built this elaborate red and green mailbox and then there was a signal, I think it was a certain song, where the parents could position kids by the windows to watch Santa gathering the letters from the box. Sounds like he hammed it up, looking delighted at the letters and pretending to drop some and have to chase them down."

"That's the only thing I remember," Tori said. "I didn't bring a letter or anything, but I heard other kids laughing and got a peek of him acting like his bag of mail was almost too heavy to carry away."

Fr. John laughed lightly at the description.

"Having Santa there but not center stage seemed to work for everyone," Simon said. "Sadly, that guy passed away before the next Christmas. They probably could have found someone else to do something similar, but he died like a week before the first planning meeting and people were emotional about trying to find a replacement. They didn't think anyone else could be as good. The pastor at the time didn't like that we had a Christmas party while it was still Advent so he took the opportunity to suggest that if it was moved to the Saturday after Christmas, Santa would be moot since everyone would have already done presents."

"Ahh!" Fr. John seemed to appreciate the logic.

"That did pretty effectively put the Santa debate to bed," Simon agreed. "But now of course every year people complain about having the Christmas Festival *after* Christmas Day and try to get it moved."

"I have fielded a few of those inquiries myself." Fr. John shook his head sadly. "When people are sick of celebrating the miraculous incarnation of our Lord, something has gone wrong."

Tori poked Simon's arm. "Was it your mom or someone else who wanted to rename it the Feast of the Holy Family Festival to keep people from complaining that it was a late Christmas party?"

"I think that was someone else, though she agreed it was a good idea. She also agreed that the name was a bit long to catch on."

All three of them seemed to be counting syllables in the pause that felt like a natural end to the conversation. Fr. John moved towards the door as he said, "I should let you both go. Thank you for filling me in on the backstory and for all your help with the festival." He locked the door behind them before heading to his car.

Simon walked with Tori to hers. He noticed a lock of hair on her shoulder that was snagged by her coat. He resisted the urge to smooth it down. Her hair was so soft. Somehow, he knew that though he barely remembered the few times he'd touched it. He only remembered constantly telling himself *not* to touch it.

"Say a quick prayer for me tomorrow at ten," she said. "I have an interview with Big Mike and Associates."

She had stopped and spoken while he was still contemplating her hair. It took a moment to let her words catch up to his brain. "Oh. Already? That's great."

"Yeah." She frowned in a way that disagreed with her agreement.

"You don't think it's great?"

"Sort of. I don't know." She shrugged helplessly. "I just feel like I liked working for Mr. Tanner more than I liked working for a financial planner. He mostly wanted someone to format spreadsheets and reports and help him figure out tech stuff. I don't know if this other place might have different tasks. But I have to do *something*. I guess I wish they would have asked me to wait until next week for an interview so I'd have more time to think about it."

"They may not make you an offer right away."

"True. But I don't want to hang out in limbo either." She let out a groan of frustration. "My mom doesn't want me to take a job where I'd have to reschedule my flight or not be there for Christmas, because I don't know if I could immediately ask for time off or... Big Mike's is closed between Christmas and New Year's so I could still go if I work there, but I could wait to interview other places or… I just don't know."

"I want to help. But there's still nothing I can do, is there?" he said.

"Just say a prayer."

"Okay. I'm sure you'll be done before I go on lunch so call me then and tell me how it went."

She nodded. "Thank you."

Simon didn't know if he was being thanked in advance for the prayer or for insisting she call him. The genuine gratitude in her eyes made him want to throw his arms around her and promise to do anything else that would make her look at him like that. Instead, he wished her a good night and crossed the lot to his own car.

Tori left home earlier than necessary for her interview. She hoped to have enough time to arrive relaxed and early. It sort of worked. She arrived early. But after fifteen minutes of sitting in the parking lot, her nerves were in a pinball game. Had anyone noticed her car sitting there? Did that make her look desperate or bad at time management? Did she have any idea how to do a job interview?

Her entire life experience had only two examples. She'd worked at a tourist gift shop over the summers when she was in college. That interview had been mostly a discussion about when she was available. Mr. Tanner had asked only a few questions about her computer skills and was convinced she was qualified because she knew how to change the borders on a spreadsheet. Tori got out of her car. Her hands trembled as she stuffed her keys into her backpack, and it had nothing to do with the cold weather.

There was a tiny patch of ice near the sidewalk, which she gave a wide berth. Wiping out on the way in would not help her composure or her professional appearance.

Big Mike's office was in a strip mall between a hair salon and a Chinese restaurant. The door was frosted so she couldn't see inside before she opened it. But at least that meant no one could see her dragging her feet as slowly as possible towards it. Tori reached for the handle as she prepared to smile at the first person she saw.

The office had no decoration whatsoever. The walls were beige. The carpet was tan, and the receptionist was half-hidden behind a gray cubicle. She looked about as old as Tori's mom and asked if she could help without a smile or greeting.

Tori kept her smile plastered. The woman seemed more bored than grumpy. "Hi. I'm Tori Stillman. I have an appointment with Mr. Thomas."

She gave a nod of acknowledgment before she picked up a phone and pushed a button. "Hey. There's a Tori something here to see you." The woman made a few noises of assent while a male voice did a lot of talking Tori only heard as a mumble.

Facing a woman deliberately avoiding eye contact and talking to someone else was somewhat awkward. There was nowhere else to look though. Tori saw a hallway off to the side. It didn't have any signs or artwork either. The woman put down the phone and moved her hand to her mouse. Her eyes went to her computer screen with no indication she even remembered Tori was there.

Was someone coming? It was still five minutes before her appointment. Tori would have asked if she should take a seat if there had been anywhere to sit. After several tense seconds, she heard footsteps in that hallway. It sounded like more than one person, but only one person rounded the corner, a man who looked somewhere near forty wearing a short-sleeved shirt with a tie and hairy forearms.

"Miss Stillman?" he said.

"Yes." Tori smiled, though she guessed it looked forced, which made it more difficult to force.

"Evan Thomas." He held out a hand for her to shake. "Come on back to my office."

She let go of his hand and followed him into the hallway. There were two doors on the side and one at the end, all open. Mr. Thomas stepped through the first one. It was fairly large for an office with three L-shaped wooden desks. No one was sitting at any of them. She stood near the door while he wheeled a chair from behind one of the desks to in front of another one. He motioned for her to take that before he took the chair behind the desk.

"How long did you work for Mr. Tanner?"

"About three years."

He picked up a pen and started tapping it on the desk. He asked several questions about what she did for Mr. Tanner, what hours she worked, and what was her least favorite task. He set a report in front of her and asked questions to see if she understood it. The questions involved very basic math. Tori didn't know if she should feel offense or sympathy that someone had made him think those questions necessary. He kept tapping his pen between every question, but he never used it to write anything down.

A younger guy put a hand on the doorframe as he stuck his head in the room. "Evan, Mr. Fergusen is here already."

"Oh. Uh..." Evan Thomas picked up the phone that had been face down on the desk, presumably to check the time. "Tell him I'll be right there." He turned to Tori as he stood. "He wasn't supposed to be here until 10:30. But he's a big client. He likes to come in for quick checks. I won't be long."

Tori watched him leave as her stomach tipped uneasily. She could hear voices through the open door but most of it was indistinct chatter. Clear words popped out now and then when one voice was louder. Someone asked if anyone was going out for lunch. A different person wanted to be reminded about column widths.

Mr. Thomas had taken his cell, but there was still a desk phone. Tori jumped when it rang. A woman entered the office. Her steps slowed as her face registered surprise at the sight of Tori.

"Hi," Tori said. "I'm waiting for Mr. Thomas."

"Right. I thought the interview was over." The woman wore a long dress with big purple flowers. She continued on to a desk behind Tori. It was the one missing a chair because Tori was sitting in it.

"Do you need this?" She stood up and offered the chair. She wished she knew how long Mr. Thomas would be gone. She didn't want to help herself to his chair or that third chair if the other person would return sooner. How long would it take for standing in the middle of the room to get awkward?

The woman in the flowery dress waved away the offer before Tori had much time to process options. "No, no. I just need to check something." she ran a finger over a piece of paper on her desk as though scanning a row of information, then gave a big smile before she exited again.

Tori returned to the chair still feeling awkward. It was possible the woman had only come in to retrieve a number, but Tori suspected she had pretended she hadn't intended to stay only after realizing Tori was there. The report Mr. Thomas had shown her was still sitting on his desk. Tori let her eyes skim over it. She vaguely wondered if it was an actual client's budget or if it had been put together specifically for interviews. Tense and bored was not a fun combination.

A man entered the office, but it was not Mr. Thomas or the one who had called him away. This one was older, maybe in his 60s, with thin but bushy hair.

"Hi," Tori said, guessing he was headed for that other desk. "I'm waiting for Mr. Thomas."

"I'm Frank Davies." He stopped and extended his hand.

Tori stood up to shake it. "Tori Stillman. Nice to meet you. Have you worked here long?"

"Oh, yeah. Fourteen or fifteen years. I hope Evan doesn't keep you waiting that long." He chuckled at his joke as he continued to the farthest desk.

The phone rang again as Tori was sitting back down. This time Mr. Davies answered it on the first ring. He confirmed that debt management was one of their services and scheduled an appointment. He had barely hung up when a different, much louder ring burst into the room. Tori thought it might be a fire alarm for a brief second before she realized it was the cell phone in Mr. Davies' chest pocket. He slipped it out to answer.

"Hi, honey."

The phone was so loud and the room so quiet that Tori heard both sides of the conversation. "Frank, I forget if you like the orange flavor or the plain for your fiber."

"Either is fine."

"I'm at the store right now so I can get whichever you like."

"Get the plain then, I guess."

"Jim and Charlene are coming for dinner on Friday. Do you remember if they like spaghetti?"

"Doesn't everyone like spaghetti?"

Tori kind of wanted to start kicking the desk in front of her to keep from overhearing a conversation between a stranger and his wife. But she figured that would only alert him to how uncomfortable she was. She sat there pretending not to be uncomfortable while the wife asked which vegetables gave him less gas and whether he wanted ham or roast beef for his lunch sandwiches.

Tori was relieved to see Mr. Thomas when he finally returned to the room. "Thanks for waiting," he said.

She nodded politely, though she hadn't felt she'd been given much choice.

He sat down and immediately began tapping that pen again. "Trying to remember where we were... uh... Do you have any questions for me?"

She asked if everyone worked regular hours or if overtime was expected and if she'd be working for a specific person or doing tasks for various planners.

"We're strictly nine to five here, which is great, and the vacation policy is fairly generous as well so I don't think any of us feel overwhelmed. We aren't looking to hire anyone right now though."

"You're not?" Tori wanted to ask why she was being interviewed for a position that didn't exist but struggled on how to word it.

"If you're wondering why you're here, Mr. Tanner was adamant that you're a great employee, so I figured it wouldn't hurt to talk to you and keep your resume on file for a while. We'll probably give you a call back if something opens up."

That sounded like a cue to leave. "Okay." Tori stood up and held out her hand again. "Thank you for your time. I hope you will keep me in mind." She really didn't know if she hoped that or not. But she also didn't know if she had any other prospects. It would be best not to burn any bridges.

Mr. Thomas insisted on walking her out. Mr. Davies had ended his call at some point and wished her a nice day as she left.

Back up front, the woman in the flowery dress was leaning on the desk talking to the receptionist. They both stopped talking the second they weren't alone. The front door opened and a man around the same age as Mr. Davies came in. Tori assumed this was a client who could distract the others while she slipped out. She was wrong.

"Big Mike!" Mr. Thomas exclaimed. "You're just in time to meet Miss Stillman."

Tori held out her hand for yet another person. She smiled pleasantly to cover her surprise at Big Mike's appearance. He was a few inches taller than her, maybe five foot nine. His build was decidedly medium. She had expected Big Mike to be very large or ironically nicknamed.

He didn't notice whatever surprise she failed to cover because he barely looked at her. His hand met hers, but his eyes stayed on Mr. Thomas as he repeated her name as a question.

"Mr. Tanner's assistant."

"Oh, right." Big Mike addressed Tori. "Are you on your way in or out?"

"Out," she said.

"Then I won't keep you. Have a nice day."

She wished him the same and pushed the door hard to get out fast. She thought she heard Mr. Thomas say something about practice as it closed. Had he brought her in just to practice his interview skills on someone he had no intention of hiring? She hoped she misunderstood, though she uncharitably thought he could use the practice.

In her haste to leave, Tori missed the ice patch she'd spotted on her way in. Or rather, her eyes missed it. Her foot didn't. It slid off to the side as her arms flailed to keep her balance. She managed to avoid hitting the ground, but her heart raced at the near miss. And her face flamed when a group of guys heading into the Chinese restaurant let out a few laughs. She tried to laugh with them as she knew it wasn't personal. Her three-second dance must have been a funny sight.

Tori crossed to her car. She found a dent on the door. Her car was nine years old so it wasn't the only dent. And it was small. It wasn't even the biggest mark. Knowing it hadn't been there when she arrived was the only reason it caught her attention. She gave it a sigh before she ignored it for the drive home.

None of the cats greeted her when she entered her house. It wasn't unusual for them to remain napping when she hadn't been gone a full day. She put her backpack on the dryer with her coat on top. She dropped her hat into her bin of hats. One of the cats had partially missed the litter box with a puddle down the side.

"Gentlemen!" she called. "Let's be more careful." Fitz was the only one in sight. He lifted his head briefly before closing his eyes again. Tori hadn't expected more response.

She cleaned up the mess, washed her hands thoroughly and opened the fridge to pick out some lunch. Simon started his lunch break at noon. She'd wait a few minutes in case he got a late start. Henry strolled through the kitchen while she was making a sandwich.

"There's food in your dish," she said. "You can't have mine."

Once she was seated, she reached down and pet him a bit, which was what he really wanted.

Simon didn't answer, but he called back a minute later. Tori tapped the screen and gave a mock scream.

"Oh, no. Did the interview not go well?"

"It was awful," Tori said.

"I'm sure it wasn't as bad as you think. I bet you made a good impression and are just being hard on yourself."

"Well, I..." Tori paused to consider if it was annoying that he assumed her performance was the reason it went poorly or sweet that he thought she was wrong. Both stemmed from him knowing her. "I haven't given that much thought to how I did because they aren't hiring. It was awful because I just felt in the way the whole time. The guy didn't seem to know what to ask me and left for part of the interview, left me using someone else's chair, and then it sounded like they only interviewed me as some sort of favor to Mr. Tanner."

"How is that a favor if there's no job?"

"I don't know," Tori said. "He didn't use that word. He said Mr. Tanner like the name explained why I was there."

"It was pretty rude to waste your time."

"He did say they'd keep my resume on file so I guess if someone happens to quit in... I don't think I should hold my breath for that."

"Could have kept the resume without dragging you over there." She could picture him shaking his head in disgust on the other end of the call, and it felt good to have him on her side. "Do you want to hear about the kids this morning?"

She smiled and said, "Of course." Simon taught beginner lessens at the music shop where he worked. A cute story would definitely cheer her up.

"Remember those boys who kept poking each other with their bows?"

"Yeah."

"I finally got the chairs far enough apart and one of them fell off when he tried to lean over to reach the other one. I tried not to laugh, but that got harder when he got up and asked me if he could move his chair."

"You mean closer to the kid he was trying to poke?"

"Yeah. I think he actually thought number one that I didn't know what he was trying to do and number two that I hadn't spaced the chairs specifically to prevent it."

The thought made her laugh. "That would be insulting if he was older than five, but I'm kind of surprised he *asked* instead of just moving the chair."

"Those Xs seem to have amazing power."

She nodded at that even though he couldn't see her nodding. The room had masking tape on the floor to mark where the chair legs should go. It was intended to keep the kids far enough apart to not *accidentally* hit each other with various instrument parts.

"Oh, and I didn't tell you before… that one girl, Emily, is finally starting to calm down on the snare. Nothing went flying last week."

"That's good for her, but I'll miss hearing about her, uh, exuberance," Tori said with a laugh. He'd been entertaining her for a while with a girl in his group of fourth and fifth grade drummers. She wanted to hit the drum with as much force as possible and drumsticks sometimes slipped out of her hands. He'd had to duck to narrowly avoid getting hit with one.

"Now that you feel better, what's next in your job hunt?" Simon asked.

"That's a good question. I've seen a few job listings that really didn't look terrible, but I still haven't sent any resumes or applications. I think my next step might be to try to figure out how to feel brave enough."

"Hmm." After a few moments of thought, Simon began to sing to the familiar tune of the *Battle Hymn of the Republic.* "Your eyes have seen the listings of the possibilities. Now your mind need only focus on your awesome qualities. And you'll fill out all the forms and then you'll land a job with ease. With God right by your side." It was corny, but when he switched to the real lyrics for the refrain, Tori felt his bass voice rumble in her chest with something that did begin to feel like courage. Simon rarely let himself be silly. He did it to give her courage, and she hoped she could keep that gift for when she needed it.

Tori called Simon Friday afternoon for another pep talk. She'd been texting him updates during the week, and he was supportive of her efforts. She had sent a resume to three places. Two had not yet responded. One responded that morning only to say that someone "might be in touch" regarding an interview.

"How is that a response?" she asked. "I already figured when I sent in the resume that someone *might* respond. How is telling me something *might* happen telling me anything at all?"

"I guess that could be someone's way of confirming that your resume was received."

"Huh. I hadn't really... um... wait a minute. Now I'm wondering if those other places haven't responded because they don't even know I tried."

"You followed the directions," Simon said. "If someone hasn't seen your resume, that's on them, and you don't want to work for someone so unorganized."

She appreciated that he felt she needed to find someplace worthy of her, even though neither of them knew how to convince anyone she'd be a good asset with her limited experience. "I wish I knew how selective I can afford to be. How do I know what's the best option if the options show up one at a time?"

"You can't. You pick something good and try not to wonder if something else would have been better."

"But what if... I'm afraid of taking a job that ends up awful when I could have had something pretty good if I'd kept looking another week. Or something like that."

Simon didn't answer right away. A bit of tension crept into the pause. They both knew that Tori hoped any paying job would be temporary. The job she really wanted was raising kids she didn't have. Could Simon tell that some of her pessimism was rooted in the fact that Mom was not a job for which she could be hired? While she liked to think they could talk about anything, she knew that was one subject they both avoided. Eventually, he said, "You don't have to be without a job to look for a job. So you can always keep looking if you end up somewhere miserable."

"Job hunting while scrubbing little crevices in the house has been so much fun, you're really teasing me with thoughts of job hunting while doing a miserable job."

He laughed at her sarcasm. "We can't all have the dream job of polishing instruments all day."

"That's true." She also laughed at his reference. Simon worked as a clerk in between giving lessons. And while he generally enjoyed his job, he thought his boss had an unhealthy obsession with seeing his reflection in the instruments. The moment was a subtle reminder that nothing was perfect. And also a reminder of one of the reasons she admired Simon. Though he tended to be serious and not much of a jokester, he kept his glass more than half full. The worst part of his job was still a source of joy. "And thank you for letting me vent. Now I'm ready to try to contact one more company before dinner. Are you sure you don't want to come to St. Jude's with me?"

"Drew just got home so my parents expect me for dinner. Are you sure you don't want to come with *me*?"

"Oh. I forgot about that," she said. "At least I'll have a good reason if anyone asks about you."

They wished each other a good time at their respective events before Tori put away her phone to finish tackling the dust on top of her kitchen cabinets. She didn't know if she was a bad housekeeper for not doing it sooner or if it was normal to let dust pile up in out-of-the-way places. Did it matter if no one was going to look up there? On the other hand, she hadn't known dust was capable of piling, and now that she did it didn't seem right.

The house where Tori lived was the same house she had moved to with her mom and sister about the time she started eighth grade. The one other house Tori had lived in was only a few blocks away. At the time, Tori had asked her mom why they moved to a house that was about the same size and didn't change their school or her commute. Her mom had said only that she felt like a change. Tori now assumed that change had to do with leaving memories behind. They'd moved about a month after her dad married Kathy. Her parents' divorce had been her mom's idea, something Tori knew because her dad hoped not to be blamed. No one had told her anything else since - and she'd never ask - but she couldn't help thinking her mom might have some regrets.

Tori had taken over the mortgage payments on the new house when her mom moved to Florida, where she lived with Tori's sister and brother-in-law. She said when it came time to sell, they'd figure out a fair way to split the equity. Tori expected that her mom intended to give her way more than her fair share out of guilt from leaving her, but she'd worry about the haggling when the time came. For now, she was happy to have a place to live.

She took a break to text her mom about when the cabinets had last been dusted before she cleaned the countertops, that were cleaned regularly but had gotten collateral damage during the dust-un-piling. Her mom responded defensively, and Tori sent a few more texts to clarify that she had only been curious and intended no criticism. It turned out that her mom's initial response had been sarcastic. She didn't actually care what anyone thought of her dusting abilities. Fortunately, the two of them had the kind of relationship where they both got a laugh out of the misunderstanding rather than building additional drama.

While her dinner was in the oven, Tori applied to the grocery store in town, mostly because it was in town. She also applied to a large vet farther away who needed someone to work in accounts payable. Her degree was in literature, but working for Mr. Tanner had taught her a few things about numbers. Maybe she was qualified. The listing said college was preferred, not required.

She grabbed her mail to look at while she ate. There was an ad from a lawn care company that also hung Christmas lights. Tori had a large lighted wreath on her front door, and she was satisfied with that. She also knew she could get her current lawn care provider, Simon, to hang more lights if she changed her mind. There were two donation requests from charities. She recycled those without opening them. They were worthy causes, and she didn't want to feel guilty when she'd already sent what she thought she could afford elsewhere.

The last letter was the first she noticed. The return address was her dad's, and she saved it for last because she expected a nice Christmas card. She was right. Though she had not expected what was in the card, a check for $500. He was not in the habit of sending her money for Christmas so it had to be related to the job loss. It was undoubtedly a nice gesture, and she immediately sent him a text thanking him. In the back of her mind, however, she couldn't help comparing it to Mr. Donnelly's invitation to come to him if she needed anything. Tori knew that her dad meant to make it easy on her, but his check somehow felt like the opposite of an invitation. Take this so you don't have to come to me. Why were feelings sometimes complicated?

That was a question Tori did not want to ponder. She put on her coat and picked out a red hat, then went to St. Jude's to find something more spiritual to ponder.

She got to the school behind the church in time to hold the door for Joseph and Emily, who had three little ones. Emily was carrying the baby while Joseph had each of the ones who could walk by a hand.

"Thanks, Tori," Emily said. "Joseph told me he helped Mr. Tanner clean out his office just before Thanksgiving. You work for him, don't you?"

"Well, I did."

"Right. Do you have a new job?"

Tori shook her head. "I'm still looking."

"I could put in a good word for you at Burger Brothers," Emily offered. "I used to work there. But I don't think Chip is hiring anyone right now."

"I appreciate that, but... I mean, if he's not hiring..." Tori tried to turn down the offer without admitting Chip was so scary she got nervous ordering a sandwich. Her heart rate picked up a bit at the mere suggestion of asking him for a job.

"He loves his scary reputation, but he's all bark." Emily laughed lightly, apparently also enjoying the scary reputation that caused Tori to hesitate. "Let me know if you change your mind."

A plastic fence created a play area in the hallway for the toddlers. Two older women looked after them while the young adults met in nearby rooms. Everyone gathered for a few minutes of small talk and an opening prayer before the guys moved across the hall for the meat of the discussion. The group was generally too large to let many people talk if they stayed together.

Once the ladies were alone, Heather asked Tori where Simon was. She and Simon had joined the group together after college. They seemed to need to clarify that they were not dating every week. It didn't take long for Simon to get tired of that. Tori still got questions about him regularly, though not every week. The fact that the questions always came after the guys left the room made her think people were hoping for a juicy update on their status more than an update on his whereabouts. But, somehow, the insinuations didn't bother her as much when he wasn't there to hear them.

"His brother just got home from school so he's hanging out with family tonight," Tori said.

Heather nodded. Her eyes had just a hint of disappointment.

"That's probably where Eve is, too," Emily observed. "Though I couldn't help noticing Ben is also missing tonight."

Tori smiled at the speculative glances. There had been growing suspicions about Ben and Eve for some time. Tori had information it was not her place to share, but she hoped Eve could get everything worked out soon.

"Okay, ladies, we're going to talk about St. Bernadette today." Ruth was the leader and ready to get the meeting going. "We're going to start with a fun question. Bernadette is the saint who discovered the spring at Lourdes after a vision of Mary showed her where to dig. Gabe thinks digging for treasure is some universal childhood thing so I want to ask... Have any of you done that, like digging in your yard or at the beach or something, and did you ever find anything interesting?"

"I dug for shells at the beach," Jessica said. "I remember my sister gave me a hard time about it because you could just pick them up on the surface of the sand. I was convinced there were better ones if you dug into the sand, probably just because I assumed other people had already picked up the easy ones. As for anything interesting... not really. I did find shells, but most of them kind of looked the same and maybe not even better than what my sister found. Though I'm sure I didn't admit that at the time." She finished with a guilty smile.

"I dug holes at the beach all the time," Tori said, "but I don't think I was looking for anything."

"I found a coin once," Emily said. "I was helping my mom plant some flowers and digging the holes way bigger than necessary because I knew I wouldn't normally be allowed to go digging holes in the yard so I think Gabriel is onto something with the idea of a natural desire to dig and anyway, I found a quarter that I was sure was ancient and valuable, mostly because it was so dirty. I cleaned it off and showed it to my mom. She was like, this coin was minted the year I was born and is therefore not the least bit old and worth exactly twenty-five cents."

Emily shifted the baby in her lap as she continued. The little one flashed a cute smile and made her story even more entertaining. "Even though I was disappointed it wasn't super rare, I was still kind of happy to have found twenty-five cents since I hadn't expected to find anything."

One woman said she also dug holes at the beach more for the fun of digging a hole than trying to find anything, and another woman said she dug shallow holes in the sand to create designs. Then Cassidy, who could generally be counted on to take the conversation in a philosophical direction, said she wondered if a natural desire to dig was related to man's search for God.

"As St. Augustine famously said, 'Our hearts are restless until they rest in thee.' Is digging part of our innate searching for God, and then we outgrow it as we mature enough to realize it's not a physical longing?"

The idea took a moment to sink in. Then several women agreed that the thought had merit while as many others were more skeptical. Tori mostly disagreed but kept that to herself. She definitely agreed with the innate longing for God and liked the idea of it manifesting in a physical searching. But she was pretty sure digging was simply part of the general curiosity of childhood. How big or deep can I make this hole before I have to go home, or before my arms get tired, or before my parents notice what I'm doing and yell at me to put the yard back together?

Ruth asked if anyone had visited Lourdes. One woman had a grandmother who had been and said it was on her bucket list, too. But no one had personal experience. Then Ruth talked a bit about how Bernadette became something of a celebrity because of her visions. Some people wanted to worship her or rip off pieces of her clothes as relics while others harassed her as a liar trying to get her to say she made it all up. Ruth asked which group would make life more difficult.

Most of the women thought that was an easy question, that people saying hurtful things was worse. But Emily pointed out that detractors are easier to ignore the more people you have backing you up. She thought that with enough people treating you like royalty, it would be difficult to stay humble and selfish people tended to be unhappy.

The discussion moved to some quotes from Bernadette's visions and ended in a contest to see how many titles for Mary the group could list. Jessica amazed everyone when she recited the entire Litany of Loretto from memory. Then Ruth went around the room giving each of them a chance to name prayer requests.

When it was Tori's turn, she asked for prayers for her job search.

"You need a job?" Ruth's eyes lit with interest.

"Yeah. I was working for Mr. Tanner, the financial planner downtown, but he retired last week."

"I thought he retired like a year ago," Heather said.

"He was talking about it longer than that," Tori said, "but he didn't actually close up until the day before Thanksgiving."

"Do you want to work with me?" Ruth asked.

Tori liked Ruth, and part of her wanted to nod. Part of her knew it was a good idea to ask what the job was first.

"I work for Ella's dad." She pointed at Ella, who confirmed it with a nod. "We both worked for him until Matthew was born, and the woman he hired to replace Ella... uh... let's just say she didn't work out."

Ella nodded again, saying with her expression that Ruth was being generous with her words.

"I've been swamped the last two weeks," Ruth continued. "Can you come in on Monday?"

"Uh..." Wheels were spinning in Tori's head. She knew Ella's dad, Mr. Sweet, was an insurance agent because she had seen his office just down the block from where she used to work. A small office where she could continue to walk to work, where she'd probably have similar tasks to what she'd done for Mr. Tanner, and she'd have maybe not a close friend but someone she'd known through this group for a couple of years helping her get started? Tori was already convinced she wanted the job. She was not convinced Ruth had the authority to give it to her. "You want me to just show up for work without being hired?"

"Ella and I will both vouch for you, and that's all he'll need to know to hire you. I only needed Ella's word to get the job. But I can see how that'll be awkward for you and not the best first impression maybe so..." Ruth paused while she processed the situation. "We have the weekend," she said decisively.

Tori didn't understand how that fixed everything, but she was excited for Ruth to tell her.

"Give your number to Ella. She can talk to her dad this weekend, and he can either do a phone interview or call you to set something up for Monday morning. Then you come prepared to stay and help me."

Ella had already placed baby Matthew on a blanket to have her hands free to take a number. The other women resumed prayer requests while Tori thanked God that hers might have already been answered.

Simon couldn't possibly be expected to know which pills he needed. His mom handled the medical stuff. And yet Simon had gotten an early morning text from Grandpa Will asking him to bring the pills when he came to pick him up for church. At least, that was how Simon had interpreted the message. It was clear enough to tell he was asking for *something*.

Simon called his mom for suggestions.

"Hey, Simon. What's up?"

"I got a text from Grandpa Will that I think is asking me to bring him some pills this morning. That's not my department so I thought I should mention it to you in case he's needing a prescription refilled."

"Huh. Lucy's good at staying on top of his medications. I'm sure she would have called me if he was low. I bet he's confused."

Lucy was a nurse at the place Grandpa Will lived. She was assigned to make sure he didn't forget any medication or accidentally take something twice. Simon had met her several times, and she always struck him as competent. "It's more likely *I'm* confused," he admitted. "You know what his texts look like."

She laughed. "He's probably not looking for pills at all, but thank you for telling me because we should make sure. I'll call Lucy to check."

"Let me know if there's something I need to do. But it'll have to be soon. I plan to leave a bit early so if there's something he wants, I'll have time to make another stop on the way to church."

"Okay. If you don't hear from me soon, assume everything's cool, and I'll see you at lunch."

Simon paced his apartment. He should have called his mom sooner because now he was ready to go and had to give her a few minutes to call back. His head had been screwed on less than perfectly most of the week. That was his mom's fault, not that he'd tell her. Ever since she told him to get Tori an engagement ring, he couldn't stop thinking about it. Obviously, he wasn't going to, but he still couldn't stop thinking about it. All the thinking had led to a very frustrating question. Why not?

As far as he could tell, he and Tori wanted the exact same things. They both wanted to raise kids in Andauk. She'd even chosen to stay when most of her family moved away. Neither of them had extravagant tastes. He couldn't imagine them fighting over a budget. And a shared faith was the most important thing to both of them. They shared it already. He was less than thirty minutes from sitting with her at Mass.

Simon wanted all the things *with* Tori. Why didn't she want it with him? He tried not to let it go to his head, but he knew he was a good-looking guy. There had been actual fawning. Sometimes it even got annoying. When teenage girls came into the music shop, he had to pretend not to notice the furious blushing and stammering and giggling, and the occasional threatening glare from their dads when all he did was point someone towards the reeds or lesson books.

The question of why not was one he couldn't answer on his own, no matter how many times it bounced around his head. He had to ask Tori. If there was any chance the problem was something he could solve, he needed to start fixing it. And if it wasn't, he needed to start figuring out how to get over her and move on.

He didn't know when he'd next talk to Tori alone. The question for her had to wait while he focused on Grandpa Will's question for him. His mom hadn't contacted him so it probably wasn't pills after all, not that Simon was surprised he'd guessed wrong on the gibberish. He grabbed a jacket and drove out to pick up his grandpa.

The assisted living place had a diligent grounds crew. The lawn had uniform grass with crisp edges and flowers along the border of the walk. To keep the color in the winter, silk flowers were attached to the bare stems. You could only tell they were fake if you looked closely, and Simon might have never looked that closely if he hadn't happened to visit when the gardeners were adding them. Pretty Christmas lights also hung in the trees and within the greenery around the front door.

Simon walked into the lobby. There was a circular desk in the center where he was supposed to let someone know which room he was visiting. His Sunday routine was well enough established that the woman at the desk typically waved him through with a comment about it being nice to see him again or that she hoped they enjoyed church. Someone new, or at least different, was sitting behind the desk. He walked up to it. "Good morning," he said. "I'm Simon Donnelly, here to visit room 121."

"Hi." The woman seemed a bit startled and just stared at him. She had dark hair cut jaggedly above her shoulders and wore flowery scrubs with bright pink fingernails.

When the quiet began to stretch into awkwardness, Simon tried to push the interaction along. "I'm taking him to church and then lunch so he won't be back until... uh... probably between one and two."

She smiled. "You're, uh... younger than a lot of our visitors."

Simon had seen people of all ages coming and going, including children. He supposed he was younger than average, but it still seemed like an odd comment. He didn't know how to respond and chose not to directly. "I'm glad the residents do seem to get a lot of visitors." He glanced somewhat pointedly at the book where visitors were recorded.

"Right," she said. "What did you say your name was?"

"Simon Donnelly."

"Simon? That's nice." She smiled at him a moment longer before she lowered her eyes to write it down. When her pen moved towards the room number, Simon repeated it before she asked. "Will he be back for lunch? And will you, perhaps, be joining us?"

He got the impression she expected her use of the word "us" to get a reaction. His strongest reaction was a desire to roll his eyes at her not listening to a word he said. He managed to resist that. "No. He'll be back after lunch."

"Well, I hope to see you again when you bring him back." She smiled flirtatiously.

Simon tried to nod in a way that was polite but not encouraging, and then he tried to walk a normal pace to his grandpa's room when he wanted to sprint.

Grandpa Will had his door open, and Simon knocked on it as he came inside. It took Grandpa Will a minute to look up from his book. He set his magnified reading light on the desk next to him as he did.

"Hi, Grandpa," Simon said. "I'm sorry I couldn't understand your message this morning. Is there something you wanted me to bring?"

Grandpa Will shook his head. "It wasn't important."

He looked away as he spoke. Simon recognized that the old guy didn't want to admit he couldn't remember sending a message. But if he couldn't remember, it may not have been important. "Are you ready to go then?"

"Almost. I couldn't seem to get my fingers around that tie this morning." He gestured to a blue and purple striped tie on the end of his bed. "Can you give me a hand?"

"Sure." Simon picked up the tie and put it around his own neck. He couldn't tie it backwards. He tied it loosely so he could slip it over his head and be ready to put it over his grandpa's head once he had pushed himself to standing.

Grandpa Will didn't wear a tie every week, usually only on special occasions. Simon watched him pull the tie tighter and straighten it under his collar.

"Am I forgetting a feast day?" he asked.

"Sometimes Sunday is enough," Grandpa Will said. "But I have been told I look extra dashing in purple, and it's appropriate for Advent."

A pair of older ladies were passing as they entered the hallway. "Hi, Mary. Hi, Barb." There weren't many residents Simon could greet by name. But Mary and Barb were gregarious women he seemed to bump into most visits. It helped that they left for a different church around the same time on Sundays.

"Simon!" Barb exclaimed, "Are you still putting up with this cranky old man?" She sent Grandpa Will a teasing smile.

"When I have to," Simon said.

"Ha!" Grandpa Will nudged him. "It's me that has to do the putting up with. The boy insists on driving the speed limit."

"I bet he only does that with you in the car," Mary said.

"And only because he knows it bothers you," Barb added.

Simon knew that Mary was one of the few residents who still had a car. "Well, I hope you will drive safely this morning no matter what speed that is. We don't want anything to happen to you."

She laughed. "Isn't it cute how he thinks he can charm us out of teasing him?"

"If we were fifty years younger, it might work," Barb said.

"*Thirty* years." Mary glared playfully at her friend. "Stop trying to make me sound old."

They had been walking as they chatted and had nearly reached the front desk. "I hope you ladies have a nice time with God this morning," Grandpa Will said.

"Thank you, and you as well," Barb replied.

Mary sang, "Praise God from whom all blessing flow," and then raised her eyebrows at Simon.

He joined both the ladies in singing the hymn on the way outside, happy that it prohibited any further small talk by the desk. They finished the first verse at the front door and sang the second getting farther apart as Mary was parked in the resident section of the lot.

Since they ended up not needing an extra stop for whatever Grandpa Will had wanted, people were still exiting St. Jude's from the earlier Mass when they arrived. Enough cars had pulled out of the lot that Simon was able to get a spot close to the door. He had a permit for handicap parking that his mom had gone to a lot of trouble to get that his grandpa refused to use. He insisted those spaces were for people who really needed them, not ninety-one-year-old men who got winded and wobbly after short walks. The tag was in the glove box. Simon pulled it out and did some insisting of his own in situations where he thought he might end up carrying someone. The church lot was small enough he didn't put up a fight.

They walked slowly as Grandpa Will paused to greet some of the people leaving. Once in the church, they were able to move directly to the second pew. Tori wasn't there yet. There were more people still standing in the back than seated for the next Mass. Grandpa Will pulled a rosary from his pocket and Simon did the same. He was in the middle of the second decade when Tori sat on the end seat left open for her.

He heard his grandpa whisper to her that she was late. It wasn't surprising that he heard, as the diminished hearing meant his whisper was more of a change in tone than volume. Simon smiled at the familiar jab without turning until some shifting next to him drew his attention. Tori had brought a small pillow, more of a cushion, that she slid between the hard wooden pew and Grandpa Will's back. The seat was already padded. She was thanked in another loud whisper, and Simon offered her a nod for her thoughtfulness.

He moved his fingers to the next bead. Then his mind connected the similar letters in pills and pillow. He reached across and tapped Tori. "Did he text you to bring that?"

"Yes." She smiled smugly at him.

She seemed to have a better success rate on the garbled texts. At least the mystery had been solved, even if someone else solved it. Maybe her text had fewer extra letters. Or maybe she remembered that pillow. She'd brought it for him when they first started sitting with her. Simon didn't know why she stopped, but he guessed it had something to do with his grandpa refusing to be treated like an invalid. After Mass, he admitted it felt nice though. He said he'd woken up stiffer than usual, and he asked Simon if he could keep it in his car for future Sundays just in case.

Simon looked to Tori for her feeling. Her eyes smiled as she nodded. It communicated both that she didn't mind him keeping the pillow or the fact that Grandpa Will seemed to be giving credit for it to Simon.

It had started snowing while they were in church. Tiny flakes that weren't much more than flurries were swirling over the black of the parking lot surface.

"Are we expecting a storm?" Grandpa Will asked.

"No." Tori assured him that less than an inch was in the forecast. "I wasn't sure we'd see any."

"That's good," he said. "More snow usually means more accidents. It can wait a few weeks to give us a white Christmas people can enjoy from the safety of a family home."

"Family home sounds good right now," Simon said. "I'm hungry for whatever Mom's making."

"Me, too." Grandpa Will let out a soft groan as he climbed into the passenger seat. "As long as it's not chicken. They make us chicken every other day out at the old folks home, like we all turn into coyotes after a certain age."

Simon closed the door and turned to tell Tori he'd see her again in a minute.

"Now I'm going to laugh and think of coyotes if your mom serves any form of chicken."

"I'll still be hungry for it through the laugh," he said. "See you soon."

There *was* chicken for lunch, but it was mixed into a delicious creamy soup that made it different for Grandpa Will. The chicken only got compliments. The same could not be said for the new song.

Simon had made progress on his song about the Holy Spirit, in between his lack of progress on understanding Tori. He had shared the music for the song on Friday, and his family generally liked it, though a few of the responses were dismissive. He knew they tried to be supportive but couldn't help getting tired of being asked for opinions. He asked for comments on the lyrics anyway.

Matt shrugged at him. He said Simon should know he didn't care much about lyrics.

James only complained that it wasn't funny. He'd been asking Simon to write a funny song for years, egged on by Tori.

Eve said she didn't have the patience to "interpret" his song at the moment. Simon had thought it was straightforward.

Drew just shrugged at him.

His parents smiled and blandly said it was great like he was a toddler showing off an unrecognizable drawing.

Grandpa Will couldn't hear the song well enough to make out any of the lyrics, but he still insisted it was wonderful. He was trying not to nod off.

Tori was the only one who actually thought about her response. "There was a line in the second verse that felt wrong," she said. "The part about the spirit being above us sounded more like it's out of reach than from God, or um, part of God. Also God? I think I need to hear the rest more or have the words in front of me."

She typically wanted to listen more than once, but Simon could tell the rest of the family wasn't in the mood. "I'll send it to you," he said. "You can review it this afternoon and tell me what you think when you tell me about the interview."

"The interview." She repeated the words ominously, especially considering she'd told everyone how optimistic she was about the phone interview with Mr. Sweet. "I should go home and start preparing."

"Preparing?" James scrunched his eyes in confusion. "Isn't he just going to ask about you? You need to study you?"

"We have mirrors here," Matt offered facetiously.

Everyone chuckled at the idea, including Tori, before she responded. "Not prepare as in studying," she said. "More like giving myself a mental pep talk so I'm not too nervous to give coherent responses."

"Mirrors remind me of applesauce. Or rather the time your mother wanted to… with the applesauce." Grandpa Will seemed to be trying to force his eyes open, his words slowed by the effort.

"Speaking of incoherent answers," Simon said. "I should get Grandpa back so he can take his nap."

As he got Grandpa Will up from the table and others began to clear it, he caught his mom with her head down to look at him over her glasses as though she was about to say something important. She didn't say anything. She did use her right hand to spin around the ring on her left. His eyes instinctively darted to Tori. He didn't even know if he was worried about her seeing it or if he wanted her to see it so he could see her reaction.

Tori had her back turned as she was talking to his dad so it didn't matter. Simon just shook his head at his mom and proceeded towards the door with Grandpa Will. Tori caught up and walked out with them before going to her separate car. She left with him but not *with* him, just as she'd arrived.

Tori smiled when Simon asked about her interview first. She knew he was dying to know if she had any more thoughts on his latest song. Sincere interest laced his question, and that was why she smiled. She knew he wasn't humoring her to get to what he wanted to discuss. Her concerns were more important to him.

"It was even easier than I expected," she said. "He only asked me a few questions, and I got the impression that... it was almost like he was afraid I wouldn't take the job if he didn't do the interview right. He asked me how long I worked for Mr. Tanner, and then before I could answer, he was like, 'That's a good question, right?'"

"So you got the job?" She could hear the relief in his voice.

"Yes. I start tomorrow."

"Congratulations! I bet you'll like the new job as much as the old one. You heard both my parents say Mr. Sweet is a good guy."

"Yeah. And I'm relieved the hunt took less time than I thought it would."

"But?" Simon prompted. The relief in his voice came through the phone clearly.

"But now I'm nervous about tomorrow."

"Ruth will be there."

"I know." Knowing that was keeping Tori from anything close to panic. "She was talking about being swamped though. I'm worried about just being in her way at first."

"I think you'll impress her with how quickly you pick things up." The confidence in Simon's voice told her he wasn't throwing out empty encouragement. He believed in Tori's abilities, which helped her believe in herself.

"Thank you," she said. "I hope I'll at least get some good stories from anything I screw up."

The comment earned her an outright laugh. "Now there's some pure optimism."

"Before I tell you what I think of the new song, I need to reiterate my plea that you start numbering them until they have names."

"I think you're only saying that to make me explain yet again why I can't."

"No, it'd be so much easier, especially when you're working on more than one at once. Then I don't have to try to describe it."

"You say that like it's hard."

Tori had a response for that. "Remember when I had a suggestion for the one about baptism and you were offended that I didn't pick up on all the miracles, that all the mentions of water were referring to the miracles of Jesus - calming the storm and turning it into wine and such - and that it wasn't a song about baptism at all."

"I wasn't offended," Simon said. "I was disappointed you didn't get it, but it was important for me to know it could be misunderstood."

"Hmm... I can't remember the tune for that one now. Did you end up revising the lyrics or writing new ones altogether?"

"No. I scrapped it."

"See? I could have just asked what happened to song number whatever." Tori waited a moment for him to protest. She expected him to repeat his argument about how unfinished songs would create gaps in the numbering. Yet his insistence on avoiding numbers had already seemed less insistent than usual. She was going to ask if something was wrong.

"Tori, what are you looking for?"

She was confused by the question as her first thought was a job. They'd just talked about the one she found.

He added, "In your, uh... your future husband?"

"Um..." She stretched the one syllable of uncertainty to show that she'd heard the question and was thinking about how to respond. Simon knew her well enough to have a good idea what she wanted. That made the question feel rather as though maybe he was trying to ask something else. Tori had the terrifying thought that he had some matchmaking in mind. She needed to discourage him from anything like that. "The top of the list is probably impossible anyway so... I mean, it's not a good time to look."

"Impossible?" Simon said the word slowly as though trying to process it. "You want like a traditional Catholic family man, right? I know a few. What's more important than that to you?"

He did know faith was important to her, and she knew that he knew her temperament and... the somewhat leading tone of his question confirmed for her that he had a specific person in mind to fix her up. A strange fear twisted her heart and made her desperate for him not to suggest anyone. "I can't... I *won't* date anyone who might come between me and your family."

"Wait. *My* family?"

"Yes. Especially since my mom moved away, I don't have anyone else. And they've all practically adopted me. Eve treats me as much like a sister as Anna. And your dad is so... dad-like. Remember last summer before you took over my yardwork when I called your dad because I couldn't figure out how to change the string on the weed whacker? He tried to talk me through it, and when he couldn't, he just dropped everything to come help me. My dad would never..."

She couldn't finish. Tori's throat clogged with unexpected emotion when she brought up her dad. Their relationship was distant, mostly fueled by his sense of obligation. She'd had no idea what she was missing until Simon's dad showed her what a supportive father could look like. She swallowed hard against the urge to cry. "No guy would understand. They'd all think it was super awkward for me to be hanging out with some other guy's family."

The line was silent.

Tori didn't speak either. Had she convinced him not to push for a date with whichever friend he had in mind? She didn't try to guess, though it could be one of the guys in St. Jude's young adult group.

"Some other guy, huh?" he muttered. Then he sighed and asked what she thought would be a good name for the song.

She realized that she'd offended him by referring to him as just another guy when he was her best friend. But if he wanted to move on, she'd only make it worse by trying to explain she'd only meant that was how he'd be viewed by someone she was dating. She didn't want to try to explain that anyway. She didn't want to talk about that at all. She shared both of her suggestions for his song.

He wrote them down to think about later while they discussed the lyrics line by line.

Then Tori asked what he wanted for Christmas, and they had a conversation almost as familiar as the one about numbering his songs. Simon didn't want to exchange presents at all because he hated shopping. She wanted to convince him it didn't matter if gifts were unbalanced. She was having fun trying to figure out what to get him. He laughed at her threat to start giving him random unexpected gifts if he didn't just agree to accept something for Christmas, but he still didn't give her any hints. They ended the conversation on a typical stalemate before he wished her luck on the new job and said good night.

Tori was smiling when she put away her phone. Even when some of their topics were repeats, she didn't think she'd ever get tired of talking to Simon. At least as long as he didn't try again to ask her about dating someone. Her stomach clenched at the memory. It was almost as though the topic made her physically ill, which was weird. She wanted what Simon's parents had. Surely there were guys out there who would understand the importance of keeping their example in her life. They probably wouldn't understand keeping Simon in her life though, and that was the real issue she didn't want to face. All of Tori's energy needed to channel towards her professional life or her spiritual life. Her love life would have to stay nonexistent.

****

The first week of the new job was fast. Tori walked in Friday morning feeling a bit shocked that it was already Friday morning. She'd kept busy all week trying to learn everything Ruth and Mr. Sweet threw at her. She was beginning to feel like a helpful member of the team. In fact, despite the speed of the first week, the nervousness of that first morning felt like a distant memory.

It likely helped speed along Tori's comfort level that Mr. Sweet's office had a similar layout and vibe to Mr. Tanner's. She and Ruth had desks in the front section with a glass door and windows that looked out on Main Street. Mr. Sweet had a separate office in the back, which he primarily used to offer privacy to clients. The door was open when he was alone, same as Mr. Tanner had kept his. There was even a similar shelf of decorative items in the inner office, though Mr. Sweet's had been filled by his wife's shopping and not random client gifts so it had a more cohesive appearance.

Mr. Sweet looked up from his desk and wished Tori a good morning as she entered. He asked if she could print out two copies of a form for him. She understood exactly what he wanted and sat down to do it.

Ruth came in a moment later. She also said good morning to everyone, but her eyes weren't as bright as they'd been the rest of the week. Tori wondered if she had overslept and had less time to be fully awake. The printer was on Ruth's desk so she grabbed the papers as they came out and took them to Mr. Sweet. Ruth had thick red hair nearly to her waist. She pulled a rubber band from her wrist and pulled her hair into a ponytail before she sat down. Then she patted a stack of papers on her desk. "These still need to be scanned and stored," she said. "We'll try to catch up on that while he's gone."

Tori knew that Mr. Sweet had a few appointments and planned to be out of the office most of the morning. She nodded, then looked up at Mr. Sweet as he appeared in his doorway and leaned against the frame, an already familiar posture.

Mr. Sweet did not have long hair. He had very little hair, only a semicircle of short hair from ear to ear that kept him from being bald. Yet he still had a fairly youthful face. Tori didn't know how old he was. He did have one grandchild, Ella's baby, and Simon's parents had talked about him as though he was somewhere near their ages. Tori concluded that he was over fifty but still several years from talking about retiring, and that was the important point about his age as far as she was concerned. He mentioned a few things to Ruth that Tori only partially understood. She still listened so she'd be ready for more instructions.

"I have a bit of a drive so I should head out."

Ruth gave him a thumbs up.

He disappeared into his office and returned a few seconds later with his coat and briefcase, pausing before he backed out the front door to give each of the ladies a quick salute.

The phone rang, and Tori took a message for Mr. Sweet while Ruth began sorting through the stack of papers. Tori placed the sticky note on the corner of her desk as she hung up. Mr. Sweet liked to come out and grab messages rather than have them left on his desk because it gave him an excuse to get out of his chair more often. It was a tiny part of her job, but Tori still felt a tiny bit of satisfaction at knowing what to do.

She turned to Ruth expecting to be handed a share of papers. She knew how to use the scanner, too, and was confident she remembered the file naming conventions.

Ruth bolted from her desk to the bathroom in the corner. She closed the door. With no other sounds to muffle it, Tori still heard the unmistakable sound of vomiting. Perhaps Ruth was not simply tired. She probably needed to go home. Tori's feelings of confidence began to shrink. She couldn't do the job without Ruth there to back her up. It was hard to sympathize with Ruth not feeling well with thoughts of how it would affect her.

Ruth purposefully avoided eye contact as she returned to her desk. She stared at it, took a slow deep breath, then released it. "I'm fine. Just don't tell anyone, okay?" Her head snapped to Tori for an answer.

Tori nodded without hesitation, though she was confused.

"Start with these," Ruth said, handing her some papers. She smiled and actually seemed fine as she continued giving instructions.

The odd behavior made internal speculation unavoidable. And the most obvious guess was that Ruth was pregnant. Tori knew she'd been married at least three or four years. A pregnancy would be an exciting surprise. Perhaps Ruth had only recently found out and wanted time to get used to the idea before she told anyone. Tori hoped she'd say something soon so she could congratulate her. In the meantime, she'd keep the secret and respect her privacy.

The digital filing didn't take as long as Ruth had estimated. She was upbeat as she started them on a few other tasks, only interrupted by one phone call. It was a quietly productive morning that almost felt more like helping a friend than being at work.

Tori didn't think much more about the secret. And most of her thoughts, or at least the intelligible ones, scattered at a surprise shortly before lunch. Simon walked in holding a beautiful bouquet of pink and white flowers.

"Good morning, ladies," he said.

"Hi." Ruth answered first.

"Hi," Tori echoed.

Ruth sounded just as surprised, but she was also grinning, whereas Tori felt her mouth gaping and couldn't figure out how to close it.

"I just popped in at Granny's Shelf, and Sarah told me my mom had ordered some flowers to congratulate you on your first week at the new job," Simon said. "She asked if I would mind delivering them. It seemed like a good excuse to check out the, uh... the new office."

The flowers were from Mrs. Donnelly. Tori got over the shock and smiled as she got up to accept the bouquet from Simon.

"Wow. I love these," she said. "Next time you pop in at Granny's Shelf, tell Sarah she did an amazing job."

"Tell her I think so, too," Ruth added.

"Sarah told my mom she didn't need to include a vase because she was sure Mr. Sweet would have something you could use. I hope she was right?"

"Oh, my goodness, yes." Ruth laughed and walked towards the bathroom as she began to explain. "*Mrs.* Sweet loves flowers. She's probably Sarah's best customer. She gets new ones for her office every week, and if the old ones still look okay, she sends them over here to, as she says, spread the joy." She opened the cabinet under the sink with a slight flourish and revealed several clear glass containers of different shapes. She eyes the flowers before picking up a round one with dimpled glass. "This looks about the right size."

Tori stuffed the flowers in the vase while Ruth held it. They fit perfectly. She smiled at Simon as she set it on her desk. "Thanks for being the delivery guy."

He shrugged. "I've been called worse."

A quick laugh escaped before Ruth squelched it, looking uncertain, probably because Simon's expression stayed serious.

Tori knew he was kidding. She gave a subtle nod to Ruth before she addressed Simon again. "Eve texted me this morning to remind you that the young adult group might be a good place to get more volunteers for the Christmas Festival."

He barely stopped himself from rolling his eyes. "I don't know why Eve is so insistent that I go to those meetings. She doesn't bug John."

"I haven't seen John in forever," Ruth said. "Maybe I should get Gabe to bug him so Anna will bring the baby."

Ruth and her husband must be pretty close in age to Simon's older brother, which meant they were only a few years older than her. Tori had sort of known that, but Ruth just seemed much older as the married leader of the group.

"Well, I'll leave you to enjoy the flowers and the rest of your workday." Simon waved and headed out the door.

"Thanks again," Tori called after him.

She and Ruth had just started going through a receivables report when Simon came in. Ruth picked it up again, but instead of pointing to the next account on the list, she said, "You made it sound like he pops in at Granny's Shelf on a regular basis." Then she narrowed her eyes to turn the statement into a question.

"Uh, sort of. He likes to pace when he's thinking, and the apartment over the shop is a lot smaller than his parents' house so he's taken to pacing up and down Main Street," Tori explained. "Sometimes he stops in various places to say hello."

"Hmmm." Ruth still didn't return to the report. Her expression suggested she was debating a follow-up question. Simon's wanderings had initially produced a rumor that he was interested in Cassidy. Tori thought it had been sufficiently quashed even before she started dating Jackson Sweet. Was Ruth concerned that he was still trying to pursue her?

"You were already working on Main Street," Ruth said. "Did Simon pop in on Mr. Tanner's office?"

"No," Tori said. Apparently, Ruth was not concerned that Simon was acting unethically. She was one of the many, many people who thought he and Tori were the perfect couple and just needed to admit it to everyone. "I asked him not to," she said. "I was afraid it would be unprofessional."

"I suppose that would depend on Mr. Tanner's opinion. Mr. Sweet is a romantic. He'd think brief visits were sweet."

"Except that there's nothing romantic between me and Simon so it wouldn't really be romantic."

"Well... not in that sense of the word, but it's still... like in the Romantic era sense of the word." Ruth's eyes slipped to the side, revealing the uncertainty of what she'd said.

Tori knew she was trying to backtrack, and she let her. She didn't understand the other sense of the word well enough to argue anyway. Ruth quickly got them back to receivables.

10

Simon hoped he'd find no reason to regret showing up at St. Jude's that Friday night. He and Tori had gone to a few of the meetings together when they first returned from college. A bunch of people asked how long they'd been dating and how long before they'd be planning a wedding and... other similar questions. He'd endured Tori's annoyance and even disgust at the very idea. He stopped attending the meetings.

But as Tori told him some of the things that were discussed week to week, he began to feel he was missing out. He eventually realized that if he'd stuck it out a little longer, everyone would have known there was "nothing romantic going on" and stopped asking. By then, however, it had been long enough that there might have been new members with new curiosity. Plus, he'd have to admit he acted cowardly. It was easier to pretend he had no interest in the meetings.

By now, it was feeling as though half the people Simon knew were at those meetings, and the constant invitations were tiresome to ignore. He'd decided it was time to face the assumptions about him and Tori and get it over with. He didn't tell Tori he was coming. She might have wanted to arrive together, which would actually make the questions reasonable. Plus, he thought she'd enjoy the surprise.

He walked to the church. The cold made him walk quickly to stay warm. The front door had a big handle that hadn't been moving at all and was super cold in his hand. He walked up the center aisle and genuflected a greeting to Jesus. Then he exited through a back door near the entrance to the school, which was where the meetings were held. Joseph Zeibert was in the hallway with what appeared to be a big plastic fence. Simon had forgotten that a play area was set up in the hallway where Joseph's mom and another woman, Mrs. Chadwick, babysat the toddlers of group members.

"Simon! Good to see you." Joseph was clearly surprised but didn't comment on it. He reached out as soon as Simon was close enough to shake his hand, then snapped the last piece of the fence. "I'll walk in with you."

The two women had their hands full with five little ones now trapped inside the fence with them. But they looked delighted about being trapped and spared friendly nods for Simon as he passed.

"Simon!?" Eve practically shrieked his name before she pretended to fall off her chair in shock.

Isaac, who was Joseph's brother and also Ruth's brother, jumped up to shake Simon's hand as well. "Glad you made it," he said.

There were about a dozen people in the room and most of them were staring at Simon. The exceptions were Tori and Emily, Joseph's wife, who were laughing at Eve, who was still on the floor and asking if anyone had any smelling salts.

A few more people came in, which triggered side conversations and took the pressure off Simon. Eve had just returned to her chair when Ben Shannon entered. Simon noticed that he made a beeline for Eve. He also noticed that she jumped up to greet Ben, almost as though she was going to hug him before she remembered the crowd.

Eve pointed and said, "Simon is here."

Ben's eyes widened with a hint of surprise. "Hey, Simon. Glad you're here. Gabriel was concerned our numbers were going to shrink as everyone got busy for Christmas, but this looks like as many people as we've had in quite some time."

Simon nodded at the observation. There were at least twenty people and still a few minutes before the start time.

"Why are you here?" Eve asked.

"Uh... are you trying to take back the hundreds of demands that I come?"

"It wasn't hundreds." Eve rolled her eyes at him. "And I'm very happy you're here. I *meant*, what finally convinced you to come?"

"I don't know," he said.

"Yes, you do," Eve said. "And I need to know, too."

Simon just shrugged at his sister. He really didn't have a simple answer for why he was finally there.

"Is it volunteers for the Christmas Festival?" Eve stared at him, waiting for an answer he wasn't going to give.

Tori spoke up behind her. "Most of the people who helped last year are back so I'm not sure Simon needs more volunteers, assuming you're going to help me with the undecorating."

"Oh, yes. That's going to be fun." Eve turned to Ben and started gushing about plans for that event.

Tori caught Simon's eye and smiled at him. There was a hint of gloating that she rescued him from the question so easily, but mostly he saw that she was happy to see him. Every meeting he'd skipped had been an opportunity to enjoy that smile. He was a gigantic moron.

"Excuse me." A woman inserted herself into Simon's field of vision. "I haven't seen you here before so I thought I should introduce myself. My name is Trish."

"Hello. I'm Simon Donnelly."

"Donnelly?" Her eyebrows shot up. "Are you related to that scary woman who talks everyone into doing stuff for the church?"

"That would be my mom," he said.

"Your mom? Right. She's, uh... I didn't really mean scary, but I, uh, hope we're going to start seeing you every week."

"Probably." He could picture Tori smiling at him as he entered the room each Friday.

"That's wonderful. I..." She trailed off as she was interrupted by silence.

Gabriel had apparently given a signal that he was ready to begin. Trish sent Simon an apologetic smile as she moved to claim a seat, though she had nothing to be sorry about. There were not enough chairs to go around. Several guys were standing by the door. Simon took a place next to them.

"Come, Holy Spirit, guide our discussion today. It might need more guidance than usual," Gabriel said, head bowed and hands folded. "We ask for your wisdom to enter our conversations and that everyone here will leave with a nudge towards growth but encouraged by your love. We ask through our Lord, Jesus. Amen."

Echoes of amen went around the room as hands drew crosses.

"Okay, gentlemen." Gabriel stood and motioned to the door. "Off we go."

Simon followed the other guys to a room across the hall. They'd all stayed in the same room last time Simon was there and it had been the teachers' lounge down the hall. He knew to expect the differences because Tori told him about the changes as they happened and liked to joke about the mysterious other half of the discussion.

Little desks – it was an elementary school – were in clusters around the room. The guys took seats near the edges that were all sort of facing the center. It was a good thing they were young adults. Simon couldn't imagine Grandpa Will lowering himself into one of the small chairs. There were a few groans.

"Should we be worried that you told God our discussion needed more help this week?" Isaac asked. He hadn't sat down yet and was eyeing his chair as though he hoped it was about to grow.

Gabriel shook his head. "Not worried exactly. Ruth and I settled on St. Stephen for the week, though she told me I'm not allowed to do Wenceslas mode this year."

Adam was sitting near the door. He opened it a crack and yelled, "Thank you, Ruth," not waiting for a response before he closed it again.

Most of the guys laughed, including Simon, who knew the story of Gabriel trying to get everyone to talk in the old style of that song for an entire meeting. He'd apparently tried to talk Ruth into it for years before he tried it.

Even Gabriel smiled. "We just don't really have any questions this week. We've been distracted by Christmas plans and... life. We're going to tell you what we talked about when we were trying to come up with questions and hope it sparks something that someone wants to discuss."

"Sounds good."

"I'm sure we can talk about something."

Several supportive comments overlapped each other. "I'm going to start by reading about St. Stephen." Gabriel opened a Bible to a bookmark. "He was the first martyr in Acts. If I read about him first, then if nothing else, we've all gotten a few extra minutes with the Bible." He read most of Stephen's speech from chapter seven and his stoning. He closed the Bible and said nothing, giving God's Word some space.

After a quiet minute, someone whose name Simon didn't know commented that he'd forgotten how much history Stephen related before he died.

"Yeah, I think it shows how knowledgeable a lot of the Jewish people were about their history, as well as their laws and customs, most of which come from the Old Testament scriptures."

"True. It makes me wish more Christians were knowledgeable about the faith."

"Many are."

"Maybe it just makes me feel that I'm not."

"And while people like Stephen had studied and could recite that history, I'm sure there were many who could not. There were even those who had turned their backs on the Jewish beliefs."

"Like Christians today."

"What questions did you and Ruth try to get out of this?" Isaac asked. He seemed to want to cut off the topic.

Simon nodded at Gabriel to concur. Knowledge of Christian beliefs felt like a topic too broad and vague to have a productive discussion.

"Well, first we talked about being grateful we live in a time and place where we're not likely to be stoned to death for being Christian," Gabriel said.

Everyone in the room paused to be grateful for that.

"And then we tried to formulate a question about small martyrdom, which is an oxymoron, but we meant the fact that being Christian - and maybe Catholic more specifically - does still cost people friends, jobs or sales and... it *can* still have a cost. But we were afraid that might be more political than we wanted, and we touched on something similar recently. And then Ruth got really fixated on the part where the, uh, the stoners, the men who stoned him, how they laid their coats at the feet of Saul."

"Ruth wanted to present a question about coats?" Joseph sounded confused.

Simon was curious.

"There were a few parts to her interest. On the one hand, it seems almost like a parallel to Palm Sunday, to the people laying their garments in Jesus' path as he entered Jerusalem. Could this in any way be meant to foreshadow Saul finding his way to the Way?"

"Uh... I think that's a stretch."

"I've never heard anyone else make that connection."

"That doesn't mean it… Scripture is deep. It does seem like he was mentioned in the story for a reason."

"We needed to see the extent of his conversion," Joseph said. "We needed to see him standing by this persecution to appreciate the miracle of him becoming a Christian himself."

"And was throwing cloaks at his feet a hint to that?"

"Maybe?"

"I doubt it."

"I'd like to hear the other point Ruth had."

Simon didn't know if he agreed with the foreshadowing idea, but he enjoyed considering it and listening to the other guys' thoughts. He also wanted to know what drew Ruth's attention.

"She wondered if there was something symbolic about them taking off their coats," Gabriel said. "Was it purely practical? Throwing rocks would be easier without a cumbersome outer garment. Or is there some symbolism of the men trying to hide their shame? Did they shed their outer selves - the part they show to the world - while they participated in the execution, and then try to pick up or resume their outer selves afterwards?"

"Well, that's interesting."

"I think stoning and public executions were common enough at the time that... I'm not sure they would have felt shame."

"Yeah. Stephen even says something similar to Jesus about them not knowing what they were doing. They didn't know it was wrong."

"But maybe it symbolizes their guilt in God's eyes. He can't forgive something that doesn't need forgiving. It's wrong even if they don't know it's wrong."

"I like the idea of it being symbolic mostly because I like when I see something new in a scripture passage I thought I knew."

"It's an intriguing idea, but I still think the coats are only mentioned to mention Paul was there."

The conversation came to a natural lull. In the quiet, Gabriel asked if anyone had any questions or interesting comments about the passage he'd read.

"What's the bar for interesting?" Adam asked.

"If you make a comment and no one has a response, then it wasn't interesting."

"I think it's interesting that right before the part you read, right before Stephen makes his speech, it says his face shone like an angel," Adam said. "Or maybe... I forget the exact wording, but it compares his face to an angel."

"Like a mini transfiguration to show the Holy Spirit speaking through him?"

"Maybe that's why they let him talk so long. With the talk of bringing in fake witnesses against him, it doesn't sound like they really want to hear his defense."

"I think it's interesting that Adam knows Acts so well he remembers a line about Stephen's face," Isaac said.

Adam adopted a guilty tone. "It's possible our sister mentioned which saint she planned to discuss, and I read about him to prepare."

"Cheater." It was an accusation laced with a smile that caused a few more.

"When people talk about someone having the face of an angel, they usually mean very pretty or... nice to look at. But I don't think that's what it means here." Gabriel tapped the Bible he'd opened again, presumably to read the verse Adam brought up.

"Angels are spirits. They don't have faces."

"Unless they... I mean, there are times they talk to people, when God is sending a message. It seems reasonable to assume they'd have some sort of face then."

"Someone pointed out to me a while ago that when an angel shows up in the Bible, the first thing he says is usually along the line of 'Don't be afraid' so I'm thinking whatever face that was, it was kind of scary."

Someone laughed and said, "That kind of destroys that pickup line about did it hurt when you fell from heaven. Telling a girl she looks like an angel takes on a new meaning when you consider they're scary-looking."

"Also, some girls won't like being compared to a fallen angel."

"I don't think that's a line that's ever worked anyway."

That comment was followed by good-natured ribbing about how it wasn't the line that was causing him to fail with ladies. A few guys shared some success stories. Isaac had met his wife in college and told her they'd been assigned to work together on a project. What he didn't tell her until much later was that he'd asked the professor to make that assignment.

The meeting ended rather suddenly as Adam noticed that the ladies were already in the hallway. Isaac walked out with Simon amid calls for everyone to have a good week.

"You didn't say much today," he said. "I hope you weren't bored."

"Not at all," Simon said.

"You're always welcome, whether you feel like talking or not." Isaac clapped him on the back as they split up at the hall. He needed to help his wife claim their kids.

Simon had just turned towards the exit when he was ambushed by the same woman who had introduced herself before the meeting.

"Hi again, Simon. Are you still glad you came?"

"Yes." He thought she said her name was Tricia, but he wasn't confident enough to risk saying it. "Did the ladies have a nice chat?"

"Oh, yes. Ruth didn't have any questions this week, but we can always talk about something. Emily said her oldest had been asking about Santa a lot and asked for opinions about what to answer. Brianna said she struggled with what to tell her daughter, too, because she didn't want to lie, but she didn't want her kid to repeat something that might spoil the fun for other kids. And I was like why is anyone struggling with Santa? He's not a big deal, just do what everyone else does. And I already have to roll my eyes at how often Emily brings up her kids when she knows most of us don't have any."

Simon tried to keep them moving towards the door as she spoke. And even though their progress down the hall was very slow, the woman managed to talk the entire time. His mind drifted to Tori. She regularly called him on Fridays to talk about these meetings, and he looked forward to it more than usual after being there himself. He was appreciating her company more in general the past week. For a long time, he'd been focused on how hard it was that she didn't want more. He'd even considered ending the relationship. Ever since Tori talked about how much she loved his family, how much she relied on their presence in her life, he realized that would be selfish.

He'd mostly abandoned his quest to figure out if there was anything he could change. If she wanted to marry someone who would let her stay close to his family and didn't see the obvious solution, there was no hope. Once his focus was off what he couldn't have with Tori - not that he'd stopped thinking about it altogether, only less - he was better able to enjoy what they did have.

He saw her waving goodbye to Eve and Ben farther down the side of the parking lot. Joseph called out a "see you next week" to Simon as he buckled a kid into his minivan nearby.

"You'll definitely be back then?"

Simon tried to cover that she'd startled him. He completely forgot the woman talking next to him until she stood in front of him again, and closer than necessary.

"Yes," he said, taking a step back and to the side. He was trying to stay out of the way as a few more group members were still coming out the door. He hoped Tricia, or whatever her name was, didn't notice he was also moving away from her. Then again, maybe it'd be better if she noticed and took the hint.

"It's not that late," she said. "If you want to keep talking, we could meet at Ice Cream Shack, inviting everyone of course." She waved her hand vaguely at the people leaving.

"Ice Cream Shack is closed for the winter."

"Oh, right. Pizza?" she suggested.

"I ate before I came," he said, beginning to walk away. "Have a good night."

He continued his walk home hoping he'd come across as clueless rather than rude, though he'd prefer neither. The Christmas lights on Main Street reminded him of watching them turn on with Tori. He looked up and saw a star in his window. She'd talked him into adding something simple to the display. He couldn't wait to hear her thoughts on the coats at Paul's feet, though he predicted she'd want to find an authority on the matter rather than speculate. Thinking of Tori so much, it occurred to him that no one at St. Jude's had asked him about her or even hinted there was something to ask. Rather than feeling relieved, Simon was humbled by it. Other people were not nearly as interested in his business as he'd assumed they were.

11

Tori opened her eyes and shook off the strange dream. She'd been lost in her own house, moving from room to room, none of which looked like rooms in her house. Yet in the dream, she'd felt as though it was her house and what she was looking for would be in the next room. It never was, and she didn't even know what *it* was.

A glance at the clock told her the alarm would beep in a few minutes. She might as well get up. Someone was not going to be happy with that decision as she felt the weight of one of her feline gentlemen on her feet. Tori switched off the alarm and looked down as she pulled her feet out from under Fitz. He picked up his head and squinted at her grumpily.

"I'm sorry," she said. "You don't have to get up, but I do."

The cat arched his back in a stretch and jumped off the bed anyway.

Tori was not surprised. All her cats acted as though they didn't understand a word she said. The three of them ended up in the kitchen while she had breakfast. They seemed to understand food. Once she was ready for work, she went around giving them pets and scratches to tide them over until she was next available for attention. Henry was the most insistent that she not stop, but she wouldn't let him make her late. She checked her phone on her way and saw a text from her mom wishing her a fabulous second week on the job.

Her mom had called Sunday evening, and they had a nice long chat. Her little niece was still cute and continuing to endear herself to her grandma. The school where her mom taught was already out for Christmas, and she was looking forward to Tori visiting a few days after. Tori filled her in on how much she was liking her new job. Her mom had already said she hoped she'd enjoy the second week, too. The repeated sentiment was encouraging and very mom-like.

Tori entered the office in a good mood. Ruth was hanging her coat on the back of her chair, having arrived only recently. She smiled cheerily and asked, "Are you ready for another fun-filled week?"

Tori laughed at the exaggerated enthusiasm. "You sound, um... peppy for a Monday morning."

The comment was not intended to refer to Ruth feeling, at least briefly, less-than-peppy on Friday. But that's what Tori thought as soon as it left her mouth. Ruth had asked her not to tell anyone, and that probably included talking about it at all.

There was a tense moment as Ruth's smiled faltered. It wasn't clear if she was thinking the same thing or could tell what had entered Tori's mind. It was less than a second before her smile returned, and she said, "I guess I am. Let's get to work."

Mr. Sweet was whistling in his office. Pleasant feelings were all around as the week began. The entire morning was upbeat. The three of them shared several laughs, including Mr. Sweet's minor freak-out over the printer not liking him and a phone call from someone complaining about a bill that turned out to be from her vet and not her insurance agent.

As lunchtime approached, Ruth asked Tori if she planned to go home. She had brought a lunch the first day, then made sure Mr. Sweet was okay with her walking home to eat. She went home the rest of the week. She confirmed to Ruth that was still her plan.

"It's supposed to be unusually warm today, near 60 I think, and I could use a stretch," Ruth said. "Would you mind if I walked you home?"

"Of course not," Tori said. "Do you want to eat with me? Meet my cats? It won't be anything... fancy."

"Oh, no. I wasn't fishing for an invitation. I have something waiting for me." She glanced at a minifridge in the corner. "I just want the walk."

Tori simply said, "Okay," and didn't question what sounded like a shifty tone.

They finished stuffing some bills into envelopes and grabbed their coats.

Mr. Sweet stood leaning against the doorframe to the inner office. "Did I hear that you're both heading out?"

Tori nodded.

Ruth said, "I'll be back soon."

"Have a good *walk*," he said before returning to his desk.

The strange inflection on the word, as though he didn't believe they were walking, had Ruth looking amused as she pushed the door open.

"What was that about?" Tori asked.

"Ella and I used to go outside for lunch whenever we wanted to talk about something private. We did it *a lot* when she first started dating Sebastian. I think Mr. Sweet assumes that we're going to talk about s-some guy."

Tori smiled, but she was not quite as amused. She suspected that Ruth did have something she wanted to talk about. And the stutter on some guy made her wonder if she'd almost said a particular guy whose name started with S.

They'd only gotten to the corner of the building when Ruth said, "There is something I want to talk about." She drew in a breath and looked all around to be sure they were alone before she continued in a rush of words. "I think after Friday you guessed that I'm pregnant, and now it feels weird that I'm not telling you."

It sounded as though Ruth admitted something and said she was not admitting it in the same sentence. Tori responded uncertainly. "Are you telling me now?"

"Yeah. I mean, I'm not going to lie."

"Can I say congratulations?" She'd never heard a pregnancy announcement with less fanfare.

"Yes, and thank you." A sudden grin broke out and confirmed that it really was good news. "I wish I could tell everybody, but... We're keeping it quiet because I've already had two miscarriages and the more people who know, the more people I'll have to tell if..."

Now Tori understood the hesitation. "I'm so sorry to hear you've had losses. I didn't tell anyone what I suspected, and I still won't tell anyone as long as you don't want me to."

"I appreciate that. It does feel good to be able to tell somebody though." She smiled wider than ever as her whole face radiated joy. "I'm already further than the first two so... I'm hopeful. We're going to start telling everyone in the new year if... Well, hopefully we'll tell everyone the first week of January."

"I'll be quietly looking forward to that announcement," Tori said. "But in the meantime, how are you feeling, um, physically?"

"Pretty good." Ruth reached over and pushed the button for the crosswalk. "I'm a little tired and have had some occasional bouts of nausea. But I only actually threw up that one time. It just happened to be at work. I might have handled it better if I'd known I might have to explain something."

Tori shrugged off the apologetic tone. "It was awkward for a minute, but I don't think that means you should have done anything different."

A car honked as they began to cross the street, a light tap of the horn. Jessica Zeibert was driving and they shared a wave with her. On the other side of the street, Ruth took on a mischievous tone and expression. "Now that we're all like bonding over personal stuff, can I ask you a question?"

The eagerness didn't make Tori wary. It would probably be a question about Simon. But Tori was used to questions about Simon, and Ruth at least seemed to approach it as a fun conversation rather than an interrogation. "Go ahead and ask me about Simon," she said.

Ruth laughed that she'd guessed. "I won't ask you if you're secretly dating or, well, I hope it's not anything terribly prying. I just want a little history. You two graduated together, right?"

"Yeah."

"Because I didn't think any of the girls in your class escaped high school without having a crush on Simon Donnelly. I mean, for one thing, I've seen him. And he's a musician and an athlete and maybe a little brooding. He checks all the boxes for a high school crush."

Tori tried to nod in a way that conceded that point without admitting she hadn't escaped.

"And you're also very pretty and smart and I've heard you sing and... the two of you went off to college together and somehow came back as best buddies instead of... It kind of defies logic so tell me how it happened."

"Well, first of all, we didn't go off to college together. We didn't know each other well in high school and didn't know we were going to the same college until we were already there." Tori reached into her memory for the details. "It was about a month into the first semester when we bumped into each other in the dining hall. I think I was on my way out when he was coming in... or maybe the other way around. We just had a minute of 'Oh, I'm surprised to see someone from Andauk. I guess I might run into you again sometime.'"

Ruth nodded. "I'm with you so far."

The response tilted it more towards a fun conversation. "This next part is actually a little complicated," Tori said. "I hope I don't lose you. There was this guy named John Paul that Simon was hanging out with - they were eventually on the basketball team together and are still friends even though he lives in Virginia. John Paul had his eye on Grace, who was my roommate. I don't remember if he was with Simon that first time I bumped into him or exactly how he figured out the connection, but somehow he knew that the roommate of the girl he liked knew one of his friends so he wanted to use that to try to talk to Grace more. They just had one class together. He got Simon to sit with me - *and* Grace - at lunch so we could talk about high school and, I don't know, Andauk stuff."

"John Paul and Grace. Got it," Ruth said. "That almost sounds like a double date though."

"Almost, but not even close," Tori said. "Grace and I ate with a couple of other girls from our dorm and Simon and John Pual brought another guy with them and Rachel, who Simon had started dating."

"Oh." Ruth frowned. "Now it's getting complicated."

"It didn't seem like it at the time." Tori thought back to what felt like a long time ago. "Simon told me right away what he was up to, probably so I didn't get the wrong idea with Rachel already in the picture. John Paul seemed like a nice guy and Grace didn't mind his company so I was happy to help. We met for lunch regularly, and the other people who were there fluctuated. I don't think anyone else knew we were trying to get John Paul and Grace together. They're married now, by the way, so that part worked out well."

"Aw," Ruth said. "So you and Simon bonded over being successful matchmakers?"

"Maybe that was part of it. Mostly we just ended up spending a lot of time together. Grace wanted to take things slow with John Paul, which mostly meant wanting other people around to take the pressure off. Their first official date was a Christmas formal. Simon broke up with Rachel right before that and asked me if I could take her place. They were planning to double with Grace and John Paul, and Grace wanted me to go. We were already friends so we didn't even really need to clarify that the dance wasn't a date. This way." Tori paused to indicate they were turning.

"Which house is yours?" Ruth asked. "I know you live close, but I don't actually know where."

"The blue one." Tori pointed again. "Fourth one from here."

Ruth nodded, then squinted with uncertainty. "So Simon was dating someone else when you sort of met for real, and that's why you're... I mean, it's never occurred to either of you that there could be more?"

"Not... um... not recently," Tori admitted.

"This might be where you tell me I've used up my question if you don't want to talk about it, but you've made me curious about what happened not recently."

Ruth said she was curious with enough hesitation to prove she'd back off and switch topics at a word from Tori. Tori had talked to Grace about Simon at the time and no one else since. Cracking open her memories made her want to keep pouring them out.

"I was very disappointed when I first learned he was already dating someone," she began. "Obviously. I mean, you know what he looks like."

Ruth laughed, then listened attentively.

"After he broke up with Rachel, I did hope he'd start looking at me as a possibility. Eventually. I knew he'd need some time. And while I was waiting - and hoping - a lot of other girls at school asked me about our status, and... maybe it wasn't even that many and I was just preoccupied, but it felt like I was constantly telling people that we were just friends and that I was fine with that."

"Aren't you still doing that?" Ruth asked. "And sort of right now?" She winced apologetically, but with laughter in her eyes.

Tori laughed out loud. "Only sort of. Now it seems I only have to clarify things with Simon to people who already know there's nothing romantic going on so it's a different kind of annoying." They'd arrived at her home. Tori stopped and faced Ruth rather than continuing down her front walk because she wasn't currently annoyed. She felt relief talking about something she normally kept zipped up tight. "One day, not too far into our sophomore year, Simon asked me if I was fine with it."

"Oh!" Ruth smiled as though they'd finally gotten to the good part.

It was a turning point in the story. "There's an important part I forgot to mention though. When Simon broke up with Rachel, he confided in me that it had ended very similar to the one girl he dated in high school. He got to a point where he realized she was always just trying to tell him what she thought he wanted to hear, and that he couldn't trust her to be honest about anything, even minor opinions. That was something that came up between us now and then. He'd say things like, 'I'm glad we're just friends so you can be honest,' usually joking about it. Like when I told him I was happy watching his basketball games on campus, but I wasn't about to drive three hours to watch one. And when I told him the first song he had published was too sappy."

"Yeah. I think we've all been sarcastically grateful for that kind of honesty."

"So anyway, when he asked me if I was fine being friends, it didn't come across like he was trying to hint that we should be more. It was like he was trying to make sure there wasn't something I was hiding from him. I had to be quick to assure him I wasn't even though... well, I totally was. And that made me reevaluate... I decided I needed to stop wishing for things to be different and start appreciating the relationship we did have. I managed to get control of myself and stop being all quivering about him and just relax and really be friends. I have no problem with the way things are now except..." Tori paused. Voicing her concern might indicate some dissatisfaction after all.

Ruth raised an eyebrow expectantly, not with the curiosity of a gossip but with the compassion of a friend.

"Sometimes I worry that we're getting in each other's way. I imagine it'd be difficult for another guy to make a move - if one ever wants to - when I spend so much of my free time with Simon. And I don't know how other women might feel about me hanging around. But I try not to worry. Surely God has someone out there for each of us." Her chest tightened as she spoke, telling her she wasn't pushing the worry aside as well as she tried.

"Thank you for sharing so much with me," Ruth said. "Gabe and I were friends for years before... It wasn't a smooth transition, but I still can't help hoping other friends will turn into couples. I promise though that I'll keep that to myself and not bug you about Simon at all after today."

Tori nodded. "I believe you," she said. "And I'm kind of glad we got it out of the way."

"I'll let you enjoy your lunch now." Ruth turned to head back.

"And even though I'm keeping your news to myself, I'll be praying for your baby."

"Thanks." Ruth waved.

Tori continued towards her house feeling that her new job was proving more valuable than her old one. She could not have predicted that when she was lamenting Mr. Tanner's sudden retirement.

Simon sighed into his phone. "At least it wasn't as bad as Eve pretending to fall off her chair."

"Come on. Noah wasn't there last week," Tori said. "He needed a chance to show his surprise." She'd laughed at his exaggerated double take and still had traces of that laughter in her voice.

"I don't think that's a need. Food, clothing, shelter... making fun of your cousin? Besides, he already knew I'd be there. He was only trying to entertain Sarah." Simon had been one of few people who hadn't laughed. But he wasn't bothered by it. He enjoyed seeing Tori smile even when he wasn't responsible for it. Not directly responsible anyway. He was still allowing himself a bit of credit.

"Speaking of Sarah," Tori continued, "she had an interesting point when we were talking about, um... there was a question about balancing Christmas gifts and not falling into consumerism. She said flowers make nice gifts because they're temporary so they can brighten someone's home for a little while without needing to be stored and that if someone gets a bouquet they don't really like, they don't have to keep it anyway to avoid guilt or figure out how to subtly regift it or anything. But then she rushed into clarifying that she wasn't trying to make a sales pitch to the rest of us and... She got teased about doing a commercial in the middle of a Bible study, but it was all in fun. Anyway, it got the rest of us talking about giving experiences as gifts, like taking someone to a concert or just doing something fun together."

"Is this where you suggest we could do something fun instead of exchanging gifts?" Simon didn't think that was what she was suggesting, but he wished it was.

"We can always do something fun, and if you want to call it your gift to me, that's great. But I already got you something." Her voice sparkled with satisfaction.

Simon wasn't going to dim her happiness with further talk of gifts. He simply waited for her to continue.

"It kind of surprised me that several of the ladies had never heard of anything like that," Tori said. "One woman was like, 'Wait. I could buy tickets to something,' as though it was a completely novel idea and... I just renewed the museum membership for my dad and his family for the third year. I didn't realize I should feel clever for giving a... somewhat intangible and very repetitive gift."

"It is pretty smart," Simon said. He didn't comment on what really struck him, that he realized she always referred to her dad's family as separate from herself. She felt only a weak connection to her local family. No wonder she wanted to cling to his family.

"What did the guys have to say about gift-giving?" Tori asked. "Lots of complaints about shopping?"

"Not really." He thought back to the discussion. "Most of the complaints were more about societal expectations. One guy said he got his wife something he knew she'd like last year. But when some of her friends heard what he got her, they gave him a hard time about being a cheapskate just because it happened to be fairly inexpensive. He's been getting comments about not cheaping out again this year, which makes it tough to focus on what his wife actually wants."

"Was she disappointed in the gift?"

"Didn't sound like it," Simon said. "But she didn't enjoy the teasing about having a cheap husband. He wants to help her avoid that."

"Huh." She seemed to be holding back a lot of words.

"Huh, what?"

"Uh..."

Simon could picture one side of her mouth tightening the way it did when she was trying to decide what to say.

"Lots of thoughts at once," she said after a minute. "I was thinking she shouldn't care what her friends think if she liked the present, but not caring what your friends think is one of those easier said than done things. And then I realized I was assuming the friends were being materialistic when I don't even know what he really got. I mean, if we're talking about some two-dollar trinket, I might also question if that counts as a Christmas present just because it doesn't seem worth the effort of wrapping it or saving it for Christmas. And yet... I still believe the monetary value shouldn't matter, which makes me wonder if I'm assuming something cheap won't last long, and that's... I was just saying how a gift doesn't have to be tangible at all. So... huh."

"That is a lot of thoughts," Simon said, "and I think somewhere in there you proved I have to get you something because even you will judge a guy for being cheap."

"But not getting a present isn't the same as getting a *bad* present."

"It's worse."

"Not if I *said* you don't have to get me anything," she said.

"Not to you." Simon believed she was sincere about trying to take the pressure off when she said he didn't have to find a gift for her. She wouldn't be mad about not getting one. But she might be affected by everyone else's opinions. "You were being indignant about some unknown present on someone else's behalf. Don't you see how everyone in my family would be all gasp, you didn't get Tori anything for Christmas? What kind of friend are you?"

"You don't have to tell them." She was grasping, and they both knew it.

"You don't think anyone will ask?" he scoffed. "Eve already told me I had to - what were her words - stop being difficult and just get her something good."

"That's not what she was supposed to say."

Simon knew that. His sister had given him an earful about Tori wanting him to agree to a lopsided exchange but that she never would have suggested it if he hadn't made her feel that finding a gift for her was a horrible burden and he needed to keep that thought - one he'd never had - to himself before he ruined Christmas and any chance of advancing his relationship with Tori.

"If she didn't like the lopsided idea, I don't know why she didn't suggest I should agree to both of us getting nothing." It sounded more like she was thinking out loud than asking a question.

Simon had an answer. "I think the guys touched on that in our discussion tonight. In talking about expectations and such, someone mentioned that there is a stereotype of guys being bad at picking out gifts and so people feel free to give us advice and even think we'll be grateful for it because we know how bad we are at gift-giving."

"Hmmm. You might be right about... I'll agree to stop suggesting you don't have to get me anything, *but* you have to believe me when I say I'll be totally happy with something small."

She hinted at another stereotype of women saying one thing and meaning another. Simon was immensely grateful he trusted Tori not to pull him into some sort of trap like that. Being distracted by that gratitude might have explained why his next thought came out of his mouth when it should have stayed firmly rooted in his head. "What if I gave you a ring?"

Tori laughed lightly. "I didn't mean *literally* small. But it would have to be not terribly expensive, or I'd be afraid to wear it for fear of losing it."

She didn't even see potential significance in that possibility. "What if it was something I didn't pay for, like passed from family?"

The line went eerily quiet. Tori wasn't just not talking; she was not breathing. Simon had let his frustration with her - and for even having this idea in his head - push too hard. She might not see romantic potential in him, but she wasn't an idiot. She knew what giving a family ring *could* mean. She was probably trying to figure out why he would joke about that. And he'd thought he was learning to be content as they were. For her sake, he needed to backpedal before she got offended or started to unravel his true feelings. "I mean, hypothetically, if I... would I still be derided for being a cheapskate if I gave you something somewhat valuable that I didn't have to pay for. Free is pretty cheap."

"Oh! Uh... well, sentimental value can be more important than monetary value in a gift," she said. "So I don't think... a guy wouldn't be given a hard time, and... no one in your family would have reason to say anything... about the cost."

She was stammering uncomfortably, trying not to say what his family would really say in that situation. Simon was the idiot. He needed a new topic to help her relax. Tori, once again proving herself more capable, threw one out first.

"There was something funny tonight," she said. "We were talking about nativity sets, and I don't remember... I think we got there from the question about how much of the gospel to put in decorations and..." She paused to sort out her thoughts, as he again pictured that thoughtful expression he liked. "Someone had a story about how she and her husband, when they were first married, had to negotiate how to set up their nativity scene because she wanted to do it the way her parents did, which was with Mary and Joseph together on one side of Jesus, and he wanted to do it the way his parents did, which had Mary and Joseph on the left and right of Jesus like they are around the altar, and she was won over by the... she called it liturgical symbolism... and I don't know if that's a real thing, but I think I wasn't the only one who thought that was kind of an intriguing idea because someone said she was going to have to consider it because now she felt like Mary might be on the quote unquote wrong side at her house. But then... this was the part that made me laugh... the one woman said, 'Wait a minute. Are you telling me that some of you set up your nativity scenes exactly the same way every year?' And she looked shocked by it.

"There was a split in the room - though with more people being on the side of it being the same each year - but *everyone* seemed surprised that some people set them up differently or set them up the same depending on... The ladies who kept it the same thought it was shocking that the others didn't see a right way to set it up and the ones who did it different year to year and sometimes even during the season were shocked that others didn't see the fun in making the sheep pasture bigger or smaller or having the wise men arrive in a different order. We all got a good laugh at... I mean, I always set mine up the same – which only coincidentally has Mary on the left – and I'm surprised it never occurred to me that some people might want to rearrange the pieces."

"I think my mom does hers the same, but I'm not sure I've paid enough attention to be sure," Simon said.

"She does," Tori confirmed.

"And my place only has that small nativity with all the pieces glued in place so I don't have options."

Tori laughed. "That's funny because I immediately thought it'd be no fun to have pieces that don't move even though I don't move mine. I guess I must enjoy the extra time to decorate."

"Oh, speaking of decorating... Grandpa Will wants to help at the church on Christmas Eve," Simon said. "At least, I think that's what he's texting me about."

"He asked me if I was helping so that's probably it."

"You know he won't actually be able to help, right?"

"He can help even if he has to sit down most of the time," she said. "He can, you know, tell us whether the garland is straight and stuff."

"I can't see you so I don't know if you're saying that with a straight face." Tori had participated in decorating the church before. She knew the last thing they needed was another person directing from the sidelines.

"The more the merrier," she said, and sounded as though she meant it. "Really. Because it'll be Christmas and Christmas is *merry* and... so it's not really a pun, but..."

Simon couldn't resist a laugh, mostly at how hard she was trying to make him. "But I'll have to take him to the meeting with Fr. John, too, because I won't have time to pick him up between."

"Right. I forgot about that," Tori said. "Do I have to go to that? You've already assigned my duties for the Christmas Festival."

"I think all the duties are assigned. We'll mostly be strategizing contingency plans for in case people don't show up. That doesn't sound like fun to you?" he teased.

"It doesn't sound like fun to have you looking at me like I can do four jobs."

He smiled to himself at her tone. He knew he could count on her to fill in gaps, but he also knew she wouldn't enjoy the festival as much if she was running ragged the whole time. "I'll tell Fr. John you can only do three."

She sighed at him. He could hear the laugh she was covering. "Noah was excited at how well the Christmas pizzas have sold. I'm happy for him and Dan."

"Yeah. He even took the criticisms in stride."

"What criticisms?"

"I think that was after the guys split," Simon said. "He told us that a lot of people have complained that with spinach and tomatoes, he should have called it the Christmas *Salad*. Apparently, Eve even put together memes of bunnies lining up to munch on it and another of someone ordering it to give the picture to his kid and the toppings to his pet giraffe."

Tori chuckled. "I did see the giraffe."

"Hey. Back up." Simon's head was still processing the earlier part of the conversation. "If you don't want to go to the planning meeting, can you maybe go into the church early and hang out with Grandpa Will there so he doesn't have to go with me?"

"Sure. If enough of us get there early, we could start without you."

"I like that idea," Simon said. "But you'll need a key. Maybe I should ask Fr. John to unlock the storage room before we start the meeting."

"Um... well..."

"Were you just teasing me about getting some of it done before I can help?"

"No, it's just... I'm a little nervous about pulling out the decorations with just me and Grandpa Will. I don't think I could stop him from trying to carry something heavy or maybe even climbing a ladder or..."

Simon winced at the mental picture of Tori trying to lift a big box off his stubborn grandfather in a heap on the floor. She was right to be concerned.

"Your mom has keys to everything, doesn't she?"

"Yes. That'll work. Sometime during Sunday lunch, make sure you tell her that you and Grandpa Will will be waiting in the church early, and she'll get the idea to come start early. She'll bring Eve and at least one of the boys so you'll have plenty of backup."

Tori was quiet for a minute before she made a noise that seemed to indicate confusion.

"What?" he asked.

"I'm trying to figure out why you want me to plant an idea. Wouldn't it be easier to just ask your mom to bring the keys early?"

"It might be, and I'm sure she'd agree. But you know she likes to come up with ways to be helpful. She'll probably like it more if she thinks she offered without being asked."

"Wow," Tori said. "I think you're probably right, and I can't decide if that's sweet or... devious."

"It can't be both?" Simon said. "Why don't we go with charming? It's very charming of me to want you and my mom to put up all the decorations before I get there."

"Okay, Mr. Charming." She only added a touch of sarcasm. "I still wish you'd tell me why you decided to start coming to the church group on Fridays."

She'd asked before, but there had been other people around. "Between you and me," he said, "I came to the realization that I was mostly resisting out of habit, and habits aren't always good reasons."

"Thank you. I like my habit of getting enough sleep, and it's getting late," Tori said. "I have to hang up now."

"Okay. Talk soon." Simon set his phone on the music stand in front of him. He'd sat down to record an idea while he waited for Tori's call. She sounded happy at the end. He didn't know if she liked his answer or was only satisfied that he'd given one. Simon was content to hear the smile in her voice either way and relieved that she'd moved on from that ring comment fiasco.

Grandpa Will whispered, "You're late," as Tori claimed the end of the pew he'd saved for her.

She shared a smile with him and was pleased to note her cushion behind his back. It wasn't even an inch thick and probably made little difference. It still felt nice to provide that small measure of comfort. Simon mouthed a greeting from the other side of his grandfather. His eyes spoke of being happy to see her.

Tori quickly moved her eyes to the front of the church and tried to ignore the warmth that flooded her chest. When ignoring it failed, she asked God to make it stop. She'd been thinking about her past with Simon almost constantly since she'd talked to Ruth about it. Memories of how she used to feel about him were starting to invade the present and led her to a scary possibility. Maybe she'd never stopped being attracted to him. Maybe she'd only gotten really good at being in denial about it.

The trips down memory lane were taking Tori to a specific moment she didn't like to think about, that time Simon asked if she was satisfied as friends. There were details she didn't remember. The clearest part was how quickly she'd assured him everything was fine, how she'd forced herself to laugh at the idea of dating.

Reflecting on it now made her admit that getting Simon to believe she wasn't hiding anything was only part of her answer. Many girls had told her they didn't know how she could stand being only friends with him, even seemed to admire her for it. Tori hadn't wanted any of them to know she was lying either. She'd been so consumed with keeping her secret that she answered Simon without giving any consideration to the idea that he might have a different reason for asking. Now she found herself wondering if she'd missed an opportunity, and she couldn't remember it well enough to search for clues.

Maybe it hadn't really been a chance to be more than friends. And maybe it wouldn't have worked out if she'd been too immature to ignore the gossip around her. But the new uncertainty was adding to fluttery feelings around Simon. Tori needed those fluttery feelings to go away before they messed up her wonderful friendship. She needed God to make her immune to him for real or teach her how to be in denial about being in denial.

The bells startled her. But she'd found enough peace in prayer to pay attention once the Mass began. She walked out with Simon and Grandpa Will afterwards like all the Sundays where she hadn't been wondering about possibilities. Grandpa Will said he needed to make a pit stop as they passed the restrooms so she walked out to the parking lot without them.

Tori was the first to arrive at the Donnellys' house. She stayed in her car to wait. It wasn't as nice as it had been earlier in the week when she'd walked with Ruth. It still wasn't quite cold enough to make a white Christmas likely. A familiar car pulled into the driveway as the garage door began to rise. Tori got out and greeted her extra family. Eve immediately wanted to talk.

"Noah and Dan were both ridiculous yesterday," she said.

"I'm not surprised to hear you say that," Tori said. "What's up with them now?"

Eve held the door for Tori who held it for Matt behind her. They took off their coats while they talked. "Noah is determined to introduce a dessert pizza sometime during the next year."

Tori nodded. She'd heard Noah mention a dessert pizza.

"They were going back and forth yesterday like 'It's gonna happen,' 'It's not gonna happen,' all day. It was kind of driving me nuts because there is no *it*."

Now Tori was a bit confused. Dan and Noah regularly debated a possible menu item before it was introduced. Why was it bugging Eve this time?

Eve responded to the question in her expression. "Noah doesn't even know what kind of dessert pizza he wants to make. I told him he needed to stop pushing for something that's still super vague, that he can't say it's going to happen when he doesn't know what it is yet. Then I asked him what it is just to prove my point and he said, 'The brilliant idea I'm about to have.'"

James and Drew laughed with Tori, though she was still somewhat confused because Noah was usually good at waiting until he had something specific he wanted before he bugged his dad about it.

"Now tell her why the thing you're complaining about is actually your fault," Matt said.

Eve gave her brother a playful shove. "It's not my fault. I posted something about wondering what Noah could do to top the Christmas pizza, and someone said something about the next thing being dessert and that turned into a thing where everybody is asking 'What's for dessert?'"

"I saw people asking that but didn't get it. Sometimes I'm a step behind."

"Anyway, that's why Noah thinks his next thing has to be dessert."

Simon arrived at the back door with Grandpa Will, and everyone moved farther into the house to make room. Tori went with Eve into the kitchen to see if they could help with lunch. Mrs. Donnelly waved off the help but engaged them in conversation about the homily while she got some biscuits in the oven. The three of them worked together to set the table before the timer went off. A rich stew was waiting in the crock pot.

Tori sat next to Eve and across from Simon to enjoy the meal. Mr. Donnelly asked again how her new job was going.

"It's still great," she said. "I keep feeling more and more like I know what I'm doing. That makes it even better."

"Mr. Sweet is lucky to have you," he said. "He didn't give you any trouble about the time off to visit your mom?"

"No. Since he closes the office between Christmas and New Year's, I didn't even have to ask." Tori was happy it had worked out that way.

"Are you leaving the day after Christmas?" Eve asked.

Tori nodded.

"But you'll be back in time for the festival?"

"Of course."

"The whole thing would fall apart without her," Simon said.

Mrs. Donnelly made a sound as though she was about to say something but stopped herself. Tori assumed she wanted to ask exactly how much responsibility Simon had shifted to Tori.

"I'm mostly kidding," he said. "Fr. John and I are going over the final details on Christmas Eve." Simon finished by copying Tori's raised eyebrows.

She smiled at his hint and raised her voice to make sure Grandpa Will could hear. "Simon said you're interested in helping with the decorations. He'll have to pick you up early, but I'll keep you company in the church until the meeting is over."

"The decorations?" he asked.

"Christmas decorations in the church," she said.

Grandpa Will nodded. He also shrugged and said, "I just go where people take me these days."

"You have to take him early?" Simon's mom was looking at him for clarification. It already sounded as though she was forming follow-up comments.

"Yeah. Either that or show up late for the decorating party," Simon said.

"We probably have enough to do it without you," Eve said. "Ben's coming."

"But if Grandpa Will wants to help, I could pick him up." Simon's dad seemed to be thinking out loud more than making a firm offer. "How long are you meeting with Fr. John?"

"Just a half hour," Simon said. "If we even need that long."

"Oh, let's just start early." Mrs. Donnelly beamed at Tori. "I'll bring the boys and meet you and my dad. It might be fun to see how much we can get done before the rest of the crew shows up."

Matt rolled his eyes at his mom. "I like how you bring the boys like me and James and Drew are luggage or something."

"I'm not going," Drew said, "so only you and James are luggage."

"Just make sure you're ready to be brought early." She doubled down on the word since she knew he was only giving her a hard time.

"Did I sign up for decorating duty?"

Mrs. Donnelly nodded at her husband.

Tori enjoyed the light conversation around her. She enjoyed even more when Simon winked at her because his sneaky and/or sweet idea had worked out. A slight flutter in her chest was fortunately quieted by Grandpa Will interjecting a new topic.

"This all reminds me of my sweet old truck," he said.

Reactions ranged from knowing smiles to full laughs. Tori hadn't heard about this truck before. Yet the reactions around her gave her a hint of a smile simply through anticipation.

"It was a lovely shade of pea green, and I had it forever," Grandpa Will said fondly.

"Though perhaps about five years longer than you should have." Mrs. Donnelly muttered the comment to herself, quietly enough not to interrupt the story.

"That truck knew she belonged with me even when others weren't so sure. One day, I came out after work - well before I retired of course - and her parking space was empty. I didn't want to call the police on the old girl, but it seemed she'd wandered off. First, I called the kids to make sure none of them had it."

"None of us would have borrowed it without asking first," Mrs. Donnelly said, this time loud enough for her dad to hear. "And there was no point calling me when you knew I couldn't drive that thing if I wanted to."

"I guess I had more faith in your abilities," he said.

Tori also thought Mrs. Donnelly extremely capable. She wondered what she was missing. "Why couldn't you drive it?"

"It was always tough because the brakes were sticky, and it didn't have power steering or air conditioning, which... anyway, by the time this happened, I couldn't drive it because the gearshift was broken."

"Broken how?" Tori asked.

"Broken as in no longer attached."

Tori felt her eyebrows jump up. How could anyone drive that?

Grandpa Will laughed and put down his spoon to mime why this wasn't a problem for him. "I just kept the stick on the seat next to me. You pick it up, slide it in, then pop it into the gear you want before you put it back on the seat."

Tori's eyebrows had not returned to normal. She'd never driven a manual transmission and had trouble imagining someone driving one in pieces.

"So tell us how the truck wandered off." Matt snickered at the wording and clearly knew the answer already.

"The important thing was that she came back. Poor timing though." Grandpa Will shook his head. "Cops knocked on our door in the middle of the night to tell me they found her. Who wants to guess where?"

Everyone simply waited for him to keep talking. Until it appeared he was waiting to be prompted. Then Drew said, "We all know the answer, Grandpa."

"Tori doesn't." Simon was watching her and could tell the story was new to her. He was inviting her to make a guess.

She was momentarily overwhelmed by the realization of how nice it felt that Simon was paying attention, that he knew her well enough to know what she was thinking, that he cared about... She turned her mind back to a pea green truck before the feeling could turn her to mush. "I don't know. Was it at your house?"

Grandpa Will smiled at the guess, but he shook his head. "Nope. She was right back where she started."

"Wait. The truck disappeared from where you worked and showed up in the same spot a few hours later?"

"More than a few, but yeah, it was the same day." Grandpa Will picked up his spoon and took a bite of his soup.

Was that the end of the story? No one else seemed all that curious. Drew and James were talking about a football game. Tori looked at Simon.

"He's waiting for you to ask," he said.

Grandpa Will was watching Tori expectantly between bites of soup. He probably didn't get a new audience for his stories very often. Tori thought even she had heard most of them.

"Did you ever find out what happened to the truck in those hours?" she asked.

"My sweet old truck?" he said. His question was an obvious attempt to delay the answer.

"Yes."

"Did I tell you about her lovely shade of pea green?"

Matt lost patience before Tori did. He said, "It got accidentally stolen," which didn't explain anything.

Tori waited for someone to tell her how a truck – especially one that was apparently falling apart – could be *accidentally* stolen.

"Do I need to take over the story, Grandpa?" Eve said.

He pretended not to hear her, or maybe didn't hear her, and began to fill in the blanks. "Christina Morin lived above the shop next door and needed some car repairs. Someone from Bob's called to tell her they'd swapped her car for a loaner, apparently apologizing for leaving a truck they didn't usually loan out but that it was the only thing left. He told her the key was in the ignition. She went out a bit later, found a truck with a key in the ignition, and drove it to work." He punctuated the story with a satisfied grin.

Several people laughed. Simon's dad said, "I still wish I could have seen the look on her face when she found out she took the wrong truck."

Tori was amused as well, but she still saw blanks in the story. "How did she find out she took the wrong truck? How did *you* find out that's what happened? And why did you leave the key in it?"

"All good questions," Grandpa Will said. He gestured to the people around him to indicate one of them could handle the questions.

Eve happily jumped in. "The woman called Bob's - the repair place - to complain about the loaner they left, said it almost made her late for work because it took her so long to figure out how to drive it. The guy she talked to was confused about what she needed to figure out, and it somehow dawned on both of them that they were talking about different vehicles. The story spread pretty quickly around Bob's, and one of the guys was friends with Grandpa. He recognized the truck."

"I wonder if she had more trouble with the broken gearshift or the headlight." Matt laughed at the picture that created in his head.

Simon responded to Tori's newly puzzled expression. "One of the headlights was broken, and Grandpa duct-taped a flashlight to the front. You had to get out to turn it on and off."

"She didn't yet have that feature when she wandered off."

"Right. That *feature*." Mrs. Donnelly smiled at her dad.

"Did you always leave the key in the ignition though?" Tori wondered if perhaps he didn't think anyone would consider that truck worth stealing, but she kept that opinion to herself.

Grandpa Will was chewing some biscuit and nodded to Eve to continue fielding questions.

"Another *feature* of the truck was that it usually started without the key so Grandpa figured it was one less thing to carry around."

"Because keys are so bulky," Matt interrupted sarcastically.

Eve nodded at him. "But he wanted to keep the key in the truck just in case it decided it needed it one day when he was fifty miles from home."

"But if no one else knew you could start it without the key," Tori said, "it might not have been the smartest idea to advertise it could be taken with the key visible."

"I believe my mom used that argument to convince him to keep the key under the floormat after this incident," Mrs. Donnelly said. Then her tone brightened. "Who wants dessert?"

She got some enthusiastic responses before she brought out a plate of Christmas cookies. Everyone helped clear the table after the cookies even though the number of bodies passing through the kitchen probably impeded the process. Grandpa Will was ready to leave for a nap and Tori decided to follow since she wasn't a big fan of the game Drew was pushing to start. Simon's dad walked her to the door with his son and father-in-law.

"I hope we'll see you Christmas Day," he said. "I expect you'll spend some of it with your dad though."

It wasn't a question, yet he said it like a question. "He invited me for dinner, but I'd love to spend the rest of the day here."

"And you'll be welcome," he said. "But Tori, I'm sure your dad wants to see you." He'd picked up on the hesitation in her voice.

"I think he *wants* to want to see me," she said, "but we both feel like I'm in the way when I'm there."

Simon held the door for Grandpa Will and said, "I've tried to tell her that if she spent more time there, it would get less awkward."

"Stop trying to get rid of her!" Matt yelled from the next room.

Tori laughed at his jest and let the interruption keep her from responding to Simon before she waved and stepped outside. Simon was probably right. Tori couldn't convince herself that her dad wanted to push through the awkwardness any more than she did.

The woman with the floral scrubs was at the big circular desk when Simon walked in to pick up his grandfather. He'd only seen her that one Sunday so far and wondered if she filled in when someone called in sick or maybe during breaks.

"Hello!" She half shouted and half sang the word with recognition in her eyes. "Merry Christmas!"

"Merry Christmas to you, too," he replied. It was still Christmas Eve, but certainly close enough to share the sentiment.

"Which lucky resident are you here to visit?" She blinked and smiled, clearly wanting him to respond to her compliment that someone was lucky to see him.

"Room 121." He pointed to the book in the hope she'd write it down before she forgot. "I'm Simon Donnelly, taking my grandfather to help decorate the church."

She picked up a pen. Rather than write anything, she reached up and poked his arm with it. "That is so nice of you."

Simon enjoyed spending time with his grandpa. He said only, "It's Christmas."

The woman smiled flirtatiously and asked if he'd be celebrating the holiday with anyone special.

"My family," he said.

She squinted at him as though that was a confusing answer. Simon knew she meant to ask if his family included a wife or girlfriend. It wasn't her business, and he was a bit cranky about that subject. He didn't care that this near stranger was disappointed by his answer. He struggled not to be rude. "I hope you also have family to celebrate with."

A small nod was her acknowledgement while she turned her eyes to the visitor book. "What room did you say?"

"121." He also repeated his name.

"Will you be checking him out today?"

Perhaps this woman spent more time on the other side of the facility where the procedure for keeping track of residents with moderate dementia made them sound a little like library books. Simon might have wondered if those residents were rubbing off on her if he thought that was possible and if he hadn't known she simply hadn't been paying attention to what he said. "I'm picking him up to decorate the church."

She nodded and gave no indication the information sounded familiar. She didn't really need to know anyway. The visitor book on this side was mostly used for the staff to determine if anyone could be getting lonely. He began to move past the desk.

"Are you keeping him overnight?" More library talk. She seemed to realize there wasn't a place to note that in the book as she dropped the pen on the desk. "I just wondered, since tomorrow is Christmas and all."

"He prefers his bed here so someone will be back for him in the morning," Simon said. "Probably my mom."

The receptionist had already picked up a phone and was tapping on the screen before he finished talking. Her evaporated enthusiasm finally released Simon to fetch Grandpa Will.

Christmas music was coming from his room. It wasn't exactly blaring in the hallway, just perceptible because the door was wide open. Simon poked his head in and found Grandpa Will in a recliner with his feet up and his eyes closed. A rather loud snore answered the question Simon had only started to think.

He moved into the room and shook the side of the chair. "Grandpa?"

A groaning noise suggested he was waking up though his eyes only fluttered and didn't open. He pushed the footstool down as he sat up with his eyes still slits. He visibly startled when he noticed Simon. "When did you get here?"

"I just walked in," Simon said. "It's time to head to the church for decorating. But you can stay here if you're too tired."

"Nonsense. Just need a second to wake up." Grandpa Will stretched his arms open wide and drew in a breath, then seemed fully alert. "I'll need my shoes."

Simon took the hint to grab a pair from the closet. He turned off the music while his grandpa put on his shoes and coat.

In the hallway, halfway back to the lobby, Mary popped out of a room as they passed it. She wore a red sweater with a necklace of flashing lights and a headband covered in tinsel.

"Hi, Mary," Simon said. "You look very Christmasy."

"Thank you. I'm collecting people for some caroling in the game room," she said cheerily. "You two have to join us. We need more male voices. And no offense to you, Will, but especially male voices that sound like your grandson."

"We can't. I'm sorry. I have an appointment to get to." Simon was truly sorry. Caroling with the seniors sounded more fun than having a meeting and dragging dusty boxes out of storage.

"Can you stay for just one solo maybe?" She eyed them both hopefully.

"I've already made us late by not being ready for the boy," Grandpa Will said, "but I'm sure he'll sing us something on the way out." He waved one arm as though he was conducting Simon.

Simon sang the first song that came to him, which was God Rest Ye Merry Gentlemen. Mary followed them to the lobby. He paused his feet long enough to finish the second verse before opening the front door. A few other residents had gathered - probably the ones Mary had been recruiting - and he heard some faint applause as he held the door for Grandpa Will. Simon waved gratefully before letting it close.

****

The church was utterly still when Tori entered. She froze in the doorway for several moments, appreciating the feeling of presence that washed over her. The church was still but not empty. And it wasn't exactly quiet either. The rumble of the heating vents was more noticeable with so few people. She saw only two others. Hopefully, the decorating that would begin soon wouldn't disturb anyone who had come to pray. As Tori took a seat, she recognized one of the other people as Mrs. McGrady, who had signed up to help that afternoon. Had she heard they were getting an early start or was she enjoying peace first?

Tori waited only five short minutes before she heard familiar footsteps behind her. She looked up at Grandpa Will and said, "You're late."

He smiled. "Doesn't count when it's not Sunday."

"I gotta run. Thanks, Tori." Simon leaned forward with a hand on her shoulder to keep his voice low as he spoke, then he left to meet Fr. John.

Tori felt a rush of something at the unexpected nearness, something that made her want to call Simon back. Whatever it was, it was stupid. Simon had something more important to do, and she didn't need him to start decorating. His mom was the one with the key.

"Are we going to get this place festive, or what?" Grandpa Will's loud whisper seemed even louder as the heating shut off right as he started talking.

Mrs. McGrady looked back and smiled. The other woman gave no sign that she noticed.

"We have to wait for the key," Tori whispered.

"The what?"

She resigned herself to talking loudly enough for everyone to hear. Before she actually opened her mouth, she noticed Matt by the door waving her towards it. She pointed instead. Grandpa Will walked with her to meet Matt. He led them to a small closet under the stairs to the choir loft. It was already open.

"Mom said we should pull everything out of there and put it up front. She took everyone else to another closet in the school." Matt grabbed a large plastic bin while he gave the instructions.

Tori nodded and picked one up as well. It was heavier than she expected. Grandpa Will noticed her strained expression and reached out to take it from her. She was supposed to be keeping him from hurting himself. "I think we should let Matt carry this one." She turned away from him and managed to get it to the floor without hurting herself either.

Grandpa Will picked up a different box before she could stop him. She didn't see signs of struggle so she just hoped it was lighter while she found a box she could carry and followed him back into the church. The woman who had been kneeling near the front was on her way out. She made a comment about how excited she was to see the transformation later. If she'd been rushed out by the decorating crew, she didn't seem to mind.

Tori passed Grandpa Will as he balanced his box on the edge of a pew halfway to the front. He assured her he was fine before she even asked. Matt was already headed back for that last heavy box. After setting her load near the steps to the altar, Tori took one step at a time towards Grandpa Will, trying to be subtle about saving him those steps. He didn't protest when she took his box and set it on top of the one she'd carried. Then he sat in the pew next to Mrs. McGrady to begin a chat.

The heavy box was a struggle for Matt, too. He walked faster and faster up the aisle, trying to get to the front before his arms gave out. He got close, then dragged it the last ten feet. He popped the lid off as he straightened and examined the contents. "That's a lot of lights," he said. "Who knows where we put them?"

"My grandson is eager to help out," Grandpa Will said. "I taught him that."

"The sooner we start, the sooner we finish," Matt said.

"Taught him that, too."

Matt smiled at his grandpa, then looked expectantly at Tori. "Seriously. Do you know where these go?"

"My guess is all over the place, but I think we should wait for your mom to give us directions."

"The first thing to do," Mrs. McGrady said, "is drag that box over to an outlet and start testing them."

"On it." Matt dragged the box to the corner of the steps where there was an outlet. He bumped it against the step and deliberately threw himself backwards at the sudden stop.

Tori smiled and Mrs. McGrady even laughed. The youngest Donnelly probably looked the most like Simon, hair and eyes a deeper brown than his other brothers and with a striking smile. But his personality was a contrast to Simon's, who could be almost stoic and didn't share the smile as often.

"I told you we wouldn't be the first ones here."

"They haven't started though."

"What do you call all those boxes?"

"Nothing's hung up yet."

Tori turned her attention to the two older ladies coming up the center aisle. They were both familiar, though she didn't know either of their names. The conversation was loud enough to suggest at least one of them heard no better than Grandpa Will. They hadn't quite made it far enough for Tori to greet them when a side door opened and James came through carrying a ladder. He banged the metal edge on the doorframe and it echoed like an out-of-tune bell.

Tori jumped.

Matt said, "Are you *trying* not to get invited back next year?"

James winced and mouthed "sorry" as his eyes searched the church for anyone the noise might have actually bothered.

Several other Donnellys entered behind him pushing a cart loaded with an assortment of boxes. A second ladder made it through the doorway without sound effects.

Mrs. Donnelly didn't waste any time assigning jobs. "James, you and your dad can wrap the greenery in this box around the pillars. Get some of the lights from Matt."

"The greenery isn't pre-lit?" James asked.

"I'm sure it predates that technology," his dad said. "And the church will keep using it until it falls apart." He was pulling a swag out of one box with one hand and pointed with the other. "Set the ladder by the right pillar."

"Can me and Ben do the nativity?" Eve asked.

"Absolutely." She added more quietly, "You'll get the most help with that."

Eve nodded and was not deterred. She'd already picked up a box of figurines. Most of the pieces were maybe eight or nine inches tall. It included the usual shepherds and wise men as well as many animals, a few villagers and a host of angels. It would be displayed on several small tables of varying heights in front of the Baptismal font. A blanket of fake grass covered everything to look like rolling hills. Tori didn't know what prep was involved in creating that effect. It took a few minutes and a few trips back and forth to make sure Eve and Ben had everything they'd need. Tori waited patiently for her assignment.

Mrs. Donnelly shifted a few boxes to empty the cart before she looked at Tori. "We have one big box left to get with the tree that goes over there. Can you help me fetch that?"

"Sure." Tori followed her out the side door. There was an elevator there that went to the basement level, the only floor where the church and school were connected.

The doors closed. Mrs. Donnelly said, "I need to metal."

Tori wondered if the loud creaking of the elevator had caused her to mishear. "Uh... what?"

"I know you've already gotten Simon a Christmas present since it's tomorrow, but... you should also give him a sign."

"What kind of sign?" She tried to think of any kind of sign Simon might want to hang in his apartment while Mrs. Donnelly got the cart turned around to exit the elevator. Tori was holding the doors open.

As they began to walk down the hall, Mrs. Donnelly revealed that the word she'd said before was actually *meddle*. "Men like to make the first move, and we like to let them because it's... safer. But good men also know that unwelcome advances are, well, generally considered far worse than unwelcome. Simon can't say anything unless you give him a sign that it's okay."

Tori was momentarily speechless. Even when the rest of the family had assumed she and Simon were hiding the true nature of their relationship and regularly asked about wedding plans, Mrs. Donnelly had mostly left them alone. Her sudden interference was surprising, especially after so long. "I... um..." She grasped at the Christmas present angle to try to make it feel more hypothetical. "A present is only a good present if it's something someone *wants*."

Mrs. Donnelly nodded emphatically, but it was clear she wasn't agreeing with Tori. She was insisting that, yes, Simon did want that gift. Tori needed to cure her of her wishful thinking even though it was flattering.

"I know he doesn't," she said. "We were actually talking about Christmas presents not long ago – real ones – and he mentioned getting me a ring just to tease me about something literally small because he knew that wasn't what I meant. He didn't even see the significance of a man giving a woman a ring because... because that's so not on his radar concerning me."

The cart stopped as Mrs. Donnelly pulled some keys from her bag. Tori hadn't known exactly where they were going. She watched Mrs. Donnelly unlock the door and reach inside to flip a light switch. It was large enough to be more a storage room than a closet. She pointed to a large cardboard box held closed - or maybe held together - with several loops of twine. It had been pushed away from the wall, presumably during the last trip to this room. "Take that end," she said, "but just slide it along the floor. We don't want to carry it farther than we need to."

Getting it on the cart took two tries, and Tori came close to smashing her fingers under it the second time. They could have used one more person, or at least a stronger person. Mrs. Donnelly must have chosen Tori specifically to have a private chat, one that she continued as soon as they were walking back towards the elevator.

"Are you sure that *Simon* is the one who missed the significance of the ring?"

The implication in the question was obvious. But it was obviously wrong. There was no way Simon had mentioned a ring to test Tori's reaction. There was no way he... And even if he kind of did, he wouldn't jump right to... Simon just didn't... "I'm sure," she said, feeling a little less sure than before.

Mrs. Donnelly nodded thoughtfully. She didn't say anything else right away. As they reached the elevator again, she said, "I've tried for a long time to stay quiet and let you two figure it out. But it's taking so long I'm afraid... I think neither of you really looks at each other anymore. You only see what you think you're supposed to see."

Tori pushed the button to return to the main church. She let the motor noise be an excuse to avoid talking. Part of her wanted to believe Mrs. Donnelly knew something she didn't. That hope was dangerous though. If she started believing that Simon wanted their relationship to change, or was even thinking about it, things would quickly fall apart. And that would spread to his entire family. Tori's Sundays revolved around the Donnellys. She called his sister when she needed a laugh. She texted his dad for practical advice and his grandpa for philosophical advice. Even the somewhat intrusive conversation with his mom would be at risk if she and Simon didn't stay on the same page.

The elevator ride was short enough that Mrs. Donnelly didn't seem to expect a reply. She pushed the cart into the church and started instructions on how and where they would set up the tree. She noted that Simon should be available to help with the higher parts soon and gave Tori a quick peek over her glasses that said there was an important opportunity in that.

The Christmas Festival would be fine. Simon knew his mom would be disappointed to hear him use the word fine to describe it. But he was confident they would avoid any serious hiccups, and that was his goal. People would probably have as much fun as they wanted.

Fr. John agreed that everything seemed to be covered. He walked with Simon to the church entrance only to verify that plenty of people were there to help. He said he didn't have much of an eye for decorating and knew people would expect him to settle disputes about which side bows should go on or how something should be draped. Those were things that hadn't been covered in seminary.

Simon entered the church and collected a more detailed picture of what was happening as he walked towards the front. His dad and two youngest brothers were working on wrapping pillars with lights and pine branches while several older women stood nearby discussing their progress.

"The cord is still showing on the top of that one on the right."

"This one is wrapped too tightly. It doesn't match."

"They're going to need to start that one over completely. It's not long enough to wrap so many times."

"I think some of the lights are disappearing in the effort to keep the cord covered."

Eve was at the center of a different crowd around the Baptismal font. She was prepping to arrange the nativity scene by getting a team lecture on how it was the previous year.

"Last year, there were too little on that side."

"Last year, the shepherds were clustered over here."

"Too clustered, if you ask me."

"Last year, there was some blue fabric making a pond here."

"I think there was a sheep drinking from that pond."

Tori was helping his mom put together an artificial tree near a back wall. They looked happily lonely. That was definitely where Simon would offer to help. But first, he stopped to check on Grandpa Will, who was the only one sitting down. He was in the front pew with a pile of lights next to him.

"Found a way to make yourself useful?" he asked.

Grandpa Will nodded. "Untangling these lights is something I can do sitting down. And Matt was just making it worse."

"Not on purpose," Matt called to defend himself. "I didn't know the plug was in the middle. I've never seen lights where the plug was in the middle."

Simon simply shrugged at him. He hadn't heard of that either.

"Looks like the ladies are about as high up as they can reach on that tree," Grandpa Will observed. "That'll be a good place for you to jump in."

"I agree," Simon said. "Let me know if you need anything." He tapped the pew as he moved away.

"It won't be more lights," he quipped.

Tori heard and laughed. Her eyes were still dancing when they landed on Simon. He instinctively reached out to greet her with an arm around her back. Fortunately, he managed to stop himself in time to point to the box behind her. "Is this where I should start?"

"Yeah. I'm already on my toes to reach this level," she said.

He picked up a faux branch and tried to identify where it fit into the tree.

"How's the... um, can I ask about your meeting with Fr. John?" his mom said.

"The Christmas Festival is going to be... good." Simon popped the branch into place and turned to find Tori handing him the top piece. It was a nine-foot tree, but it was still a stretch to get those two feet or so when the base was so wide. He checked the bottom as he stepped back to make sure he hadn't bent anything.

Tori was smiling expectantly at him. What did she expect? Simon glanced at his mom. She was surveying the tree in a way that suggested she was deliberately not looking at him. Tori mouthed, "And?"

It seemed that good wasn't enough information for his mom. He reported that all the supplies had arrived and that reliable volunteers were in charge of most areas. "I still have you as my primary backup. Fr. John successfully turned away both guys who wanted to dress up as Santa. I believe everything will run smoothly."

His mom gave him a quick nod but continued to examine the tree, moving a few branches to fill in bare spots. Tori gave him a smile full of gratitude. It sparked another impulse to hug her or maybe... He folded his arms across his chest. "Are we ready for lights?"

"We have three strings here," Tori said, "and Grandpa Will should have the last one untangled by the time we're ready for it. I'll start at the bottom and you take over halfway up?"

Simon nodded and positioned himself to feed the lights to her. Bits of the other decorating seeped into their quiet cooperation.

"Last year, that grass wasn't all the way to the floor."

"I think the hills were smaller last year."

"James, that has to go higher, at least six inches."

"The greenery is covering the lights again, Matt. Push them through it."

"I think even Simon will need a stepladder for the bows. Let me go find one." That was Simon's mom. She moved through the side door after letting them know why.

"Not so high, James."

"The third and fourth wraps are too close together now."

"This reminds me of baseball," Grandpa Will said. "Dan played from the time he was real little. I think he must have been about eleven when he started to lose patience with parents yelling directions from the stands. There was one game he was on second base and he heard people yelling go and others yelling stay at the same time. He just stood there and glared at the stands. Then someone noticed he'd stepped off the base, and the other team was yelling, too. In the midst of it all, he just calmly stretched his foot back onto the base without stopping the glare. He eventually made it home and proved to a few people he didn't need the advice. Didn't stop anyone from shouting it, but he got better at tuning it out."

"I guess that helps him tune out Noah's pizza suggestions," Tori said. So only Simon could hear, she added, "Baseball," with a glance over his shoulder that told him she was amused to see the connection.

"I had one of those Christmas pizzas, and the cute reindeer picture is still on my refrigerator." One of the women near James and Matt smiled at Grandpa Will, then asked him if things were looking symmetrical from where he sat.

"You all are doing a great job," he said. "Gets me excited for the Christmas Mass, though at my age I can't help but wonder if it'll be my last one."

Simon was only vaguely aware of a few others commiserating with the sentiment. His attention was on Tori's suddenly rigid back. She turned and whispered, "I hate when he talks like that."

He nodded because he knew.

"But I only hate it because it's true." She let go of the lights. "I'll get the other string."

Simon took over where Tori left off while he continued to listen to the talk around him. Tori was asking some follow-up questions about Dan's baseball career. His dad and brothers had finally finished wrapping the pillars and had moved on to placing some branches above and behind the tabernacle. Their instructions included more than one reminder not to let the lights get buried in the greenery.

The side door opened only a few inches. It slowly opened farther as Simon's mom backed in with a small folded ladder hooked on one arm and a big wreath on the other.

"Let me help with that wreath, Mom." Matt rushed over and took it from her. He shot a look back at James to gloat over his escape. She directed him towards the front to wait for her while she set the stepladder next to Simon and got some stragglers started putting swags on the ends of the pews.

"Last year, we hung those on alternating sides of the aisle rather than in pairs."

"Oh." The woman and her two kids - who might have been about ten and twelve - were hanging them in pairs every other pew as Simon's mom had instructed them. She turned towards the back for some help in answering the well-meaning accusation.

"Mrs. Donnelly told us to do it this way," her older girl said.

One of the other women who'd been helping landscape the nativity scene joined the debate. "I think we did do it alternating last year, but most of us thought it looked better in pairs and that we should go back to that way this year."

"Really? I think I remember it the other way."

The younger woman at the center of the debate stood in the middle of the aisle holding a lovely red and green bow with a bewildered expression while both of her kids asked her what to do.

"If Fr. John was here, we could get him to decide."

"I know. Finish this way and we'll take a picture, then we rearrange and take a picture of them alternating, then we'll text both to Fr. John." The second woman already had her phone out for the pictures.

Simon turned his back on the discussion so no one could see him rolling his eyes.

Tori stepped up next to him with the last of the lights. As he took them, he whispered to her how the priest had specifically wanted to avoid being asked to settle decorating disputes.

"What if he's not available to answer right away?" The woman with the kids hadn't resumed decorating. Something in her voice suggested she thought texting the pastor was a bad idea, but she didn't want to say that.

Simon thought he should help her, but he didn't want to tell either of the older women - who really were just trying to help the church look nice - that they should leave her alone.

Tori slipped her phone from her pocket. "Your mom is right outside," she said. "I'll ask her to come in and pull rank or something."

There were situations where a twenty-six-year-old guy would feel silly asking his mom for help. This was not one of them. Especially since he wasn't asking, Tori was.

She breezed up the aisle barely a minute later and casually asked how everything was going.

One of the kids said, "We don't know where to put these."

One of the two older ladies - who were still wishing Fr. John was there to give his insight - explained the difficulty to Simon's mom. "I thought we had the pew decorations on alternating sides last year because people didn't like them in pairs. But Eileen insists it was the other way around, and I'm the one remembering wrong."

The other woman, Eileen apparently, was swiping madly on her phone screen. "I'm sure I took pictures last year, but I have too many pictures on here to find anything."

"Well, I don't think Fr. John will mind either way both because he wasn't here last year and because the only thing he said to me about the decorations was to make sure nothing was flashing." Simon's mom paused to allow for some nodding and exclamations that flashing lights in the church would be the worst. She moved on from that moment of unity. "Let's just go with the will of the people based on the small sample here? Raise your hand if you prefer the swag in pairs like we've started."

Several hands went up, including Tori's. Simon raised his since his preference was whatever Tori liked. Her eyes watched his hand with amusement. She seemed to know and appreciate his reason for voting.

"Okay. If you think they'd be better alternating sides, raise your hand."

The younger kid raised her hand and so did Eve. Ben lifted his a second behind Eve, and Simon found his opinion of the guy lifting as well.

"Looks decisive."

Pew decorating resumed with a few sighs of relief. Other than the lights, the trees at the front of the church only had silver and gold bows. Tori had begun adding those while Simon got the very top lit.

"I found one of the nativity!" Eileen hurried over to show a picture to those working on building it.

Listening to Eve try to sound interested in seeing the previous version was probably what distracted Simon. He stepped off the ladder and right into Tori. She stumbled and let out a startled cry before she grabbed hold of his arm to keep from falling.

"Sorry," he said. It was a reflex. He was sorry he'd bumped into her. He was not sorry it left her clinging to him.

"I almost grabbed the tree," she said, laughing but slightly wide-eyed. "I'm pretty sure that would have pulled it down on top of me. I'm glad you're sturdier." She patted his arm as she let go.

The tree had a simple base that lived next door to flimsy. Saying he was sturdier wasn't so much a compliment as a statement of the obvious. Yet Tori noticing that obvious fact still puffed his ego. He allowed his mind to replay the feel of her hands on his arm. It spawned an odd fantasy of Tori holding his arm a little closer to the elbow with the priest standing in front of them. A wedding scene wasn't odd by itself, he'd actually been picturing it more often since he'd tried to stop. But he could never picture her in a wedding dress, only things he'd seen before. She was wearing that pink dress she wore to church now and then. She looked amazing in that dress. Something about the color made her smile appear brighter. Something about the skirt seemed to require more attention. She'd fan it out as she sat and smooth it when she turned. In some way he didn't understand, it added graceful movements to most of what she did. He'd have no problem if she wanted to get married in that dress, not that she'd...

"Simon!" Tori was waving at him as though that was not the first time she'd said his name.

He pulled himself into the moment. "Yes?"

"I said... Can you put together the smaller tree and maybe try to get your grandpa involved in the positioning? He looks bored." She sent a sympathetic glance over his shoulder.

Simon's eyes followed hers. Grandpa Will was still in the front pew. He was watching the people still working on the nativity scene. There were enough people around it that he probably couldn't see what they were doing. And he probably couldn't hear half the comments about how to set it up either. Simon's dad and brothers were not in sight. He guessed they had taken the ladder outside.

Simon called out to get Grandpa Will's attention as he secured the center pole for the smaller tree. This one was shorter than him. "Does this look good here or should it be a little forward of the big tree?"

"Hard to tell when it doesn't look like a tree yet."

"Good point." He stuck the branches in quickly and asked again as he fanned them out.

"Looks good there," Grandpa Will said, though there was little enthusiasm in his voice.

From the expression on Tori's face, she noticed that, too. "I already tried to get his opinion on these bows," she said, "and he insisted I have a better eye for it than he does."

Simon wondered if he should offer to drive him back. That reminded him what had been happening there when they left, and it gave him a better idea. "Hey, Grandpa, we should sing carols while we decorate, shouldn't we?"

"Yes!" It was Eve who answered.

Grandpa Will did perk up though.

"What do you want to start with?" Simon was still talking to his grandpa, but his sister sill answered.

"*O Holy Night.* You and Tori need to sing that one for us first, then the rest of us can join some others."

"I think the girl makes a good point," Grandpa Will said.

Simon felt his forehead wrinkle as he tried to figure out if he was joking or had misheard something Eve said as an actual point.

Then Grandpa Will grinned at the confusion and at the women around Eve who were nodding at Simon expectantly.

"That is one of my favorites," Tori said.

Simon didn't need more convincing, but her opinion still helped. He began the song, and she joined him within a few words. She kept watching him to lead the pacing. The few minutes of Tori following him with her beautiful voice was Simon's favorite part of the afternoon. They received grateful applause that, fortunately, didn't go overboard.

Grandpa Will picked up a hymnal to start suggesting carols, and most of the people there sang along. They moved through the songs quickly as Grandpa Will had to supply the lines after the first verse for some of them. The decorating moved along faster while they were singing. Simon was helping his mom stack empty boxes and put away supplies almost too soon. There were a few Christmas songs he would have liked to sing. Lots of shouts of "Merry Christmas" and "See you soon," were exchanged as the crowd broke up. Simon walked out of the church with Grandpa Will on one side and Tori on the other.

"Carols were a great idea," she said.

Grandpa Will smiled and joked, "He could have thought of it sooner though."

Tori laughed. "That would have been nice. I like singing with Simon because he makes me sound good."

"*You* make you sound good," Simon said.

"Relax." She sent a light elbow into his side. "I'm not disparaging myself or anything. I just meant our voices blend well."

"In that case, it's only fair I make you sound good after all the times you make me look good."

Tori raised her eyebrows as though she was about to challenge him to name a time.

Grandpa Will jumped in before she said anything. "When you make each other look good, that's when you know you've found *the one*."

Simon moved ahead to get the door. He prepared himself to hear yet again that there was nothing romantic between him and Tori. She typically went easier on Grandpa Will, presumably because of his age. But this time she didn't even correct him. She walked through the door somewhat lost in thought, and her eyes darted to Simon and back in a way that was almost... speculative?

Was it possible she no longer thought of him as completely out of the question? And more importantly, was there anything he could do to nudge her further along that train of thought? It was Simon's new favorite part of the afternoon.

Tori's first celebration of Christmas was the best. She met Simon and Grandpa Will for Mass. When she told Grandpa Will he was late, he teased her about the lopsided Christmas tree someone had set up even though it was perfectly straight. Afterwards, they went to the Donnellys' home for an elaborate brunch. Eggs, pancakes, sausage and bacon were all dipped in blueberry syrup. Tori had experienced their traditional feast the last two years before spending the day with her mom. She'd been a little hesitant about the egg and blueberry combination. This year she looked forward to it.

Everyone seemed to like the gifts she'd picked out for them. Simon smiled at the book of sheet music she gave him, mostly the fact that she'd numbered the pages for him. He still wasn't going to refer to the songs by those numbers.

Simon's present to her was also for the rest of the family. He wrote and played a silly Christmas song about how horrible it was to shop for presents. Tori's favorite line rhymed three trips to the mall with how he'd rather muck out a stall. He generally took his music seriously because he wanted others to do the same. She enjoyed watching him relax into a few light moments.

The afternoon disappeared in favor of games and conversations and candy canes dipped in hot chocolate. Tori tried not to feel reluctant when she left to visit her dad and his family. Dinner was delicious, and she said as much. Her compliment felt perfunctory rather than sincere even though she was sincere. The young girls said very little and left the table as soon as they finished eating. His wife flittered about cleaning up after the meal. She paused awkwardly every time she returned to the dining room for a plate or serving dish. Tori knew she wanted to give her time alone with her dad, but she also didn't want to appear to be avoiding her. Tori did not stay late. Her dad pressed a card into her hand at the door, and she expected to find a gift card of some kind later, probably picked out by his wife.

Her flight to Florida was too early the next morning. Tori tried to sleep on the plane but failed. Her mom picked her up at the airport, and she spent the next two days living out of a suitcase on the couch outside her mom's bedroom in her sister's house. Her little niece was the center of attention most of the visit, though they did see a Christmas light show the first evening.

Tori was glad to have the time with her family but just as glad to be home again. Fitz, George and Henry missed her. The three gentlemen followed her closely while she put down her luggage and two of them circled her as she squatted to pet them while Fitz flopped on his side to expose plenty of surface area for her.

"This would be easier if I had three hands. Then I wouldn't have to alternate who I'm petting." She smiled and moved one hand to Fitz as Henry went behind her again. "Although with the circling, it almost feels as though you're trying to take turns."

The rumble of purrs surrounded Tori with a feeling of welcome and a reluctance to do anything else. "I only have a few hours before the Christmas Festival," she told the cats, who continued to bask in her attention. "I should really get unpacked and organized for that. But you're all so cute and soft."

Fitz mashed his face against her knee in a clear insistence that she was exactly where she belonged. Tori let herself sink all the way to sitting on the floor. She imagined telling Simon that she couldn't help out after all because the cats needed attention. Henry stepped into her lap and began to knead.

"Ow. Time to trim some claws." She was used to occasional pokes and allowed him to continue anyway. She knew that even if she took the time to trim three sets of claws, the cats would be well tended before she needed to leave.

Somewhere in her head was the recurring thought that everything seemed to make her imagine talking to Simon, unless of course she was already talking to him.

That wasn't anything new. And yet... it was different.

"People have been more, um, aggressive about their hints that Simon and I... Do you know what my mom said on the way to the airport?" Tori paused a moment, as though one of the cats might answer or express interest. She took them staying close as interest. "She said she expected to come to Ohio for a wedding before I visit next Christmas. I just kind of rolled my eyes, but she was like... You and Simon can't ignore what everyone else sees much longer, and you'll move fast when you do see it. She said we suit. Of course I tried to distract her with teasing that she's been reading too many historical romances to use that word. But then she went on about how the modern tension of *defining the relationship* was how we got stuck in a friend rut and..."

Henry settled in to go to sleep, and George stretched out on the floor slightly out of reach. "You're going to have to move if you want me to keep petting you," she said. Fitz was still purring and rubbing his face along her elbow and forearm, which was also an awkward place to reach.

"You guys know I'm being generous when I say people are *hinting* about me and Simon. Mrs. Donnelly already got in my head, and now my mom has made it worse. When I think about Simon, which is a lot, I'm starting to wonder if I'm missing something. And I'm only telling you this part because I'm swearing you to secrecy." The cats got a stern look to make sure they understood that point. "It's all starting to make me hope I'm missing something, and I don't know what to do with that. I can't just say, 'Hey, Simon, your mom said...'"

Tori burst out with a laugh that made both Henry and George jerk their heads up. She got control of herself and apologized to the cats for startling them. It was stress relieving to pour out her ridiculous thoughts to creatures who were incapable of judging or laughing at her. "I can't tell him his mom said he's in love with me and not because she didn't say those exact words. She said he wants me to let him know it's okay to... say something? And she actually might have meant... I can't stop myself from thinking that she actually meant... he might want to kiss me."

She winced at saying that out loud, then felt childish for wincing. "It's just weird to think about because I've known him so long without... and weird or not, I can't honestly say I hate the idea. I wouldn't let myself think about it except... The other thing Simon's mom said was that *he* wasn't the one who missed the significance of him suggesting a ring. I almost want to ask Simon about that because I don't like the thought of him thinking I'm a complete moron for missing that. But what does that say about me thinking he missed it? And thinking about this possibility - that

Simon is not a moron because he's not - makes me reconsider a bit ago when I thought he was asking me questions to try to set me up with someone. What if he wanted to set me up with... himself?"

Tori groaned in frustration. "Now we come to the downside of talking to you, gentlemen. You are all excellent listeners, but none of you can give me advice." She was still absently stroking Henry on her lap. He and George were both asleep now and Fitz had wandered to the other side of the room. They weren't quite as attentive as she gave them credit for.

"All of this is messing with my head," Tori continued. "I keep thinking I might not know what I think I know and wondering if I can see what other people see if I catch Simon looking at me. I mean, that's something people say, right? 'I could tell by the way he looked at her.' I feel like I've heard that a lot. But I don't know... If there was something special, I would have noticed it by now unless it only happens when I'm not looking and I can't see something I'm not looking at and... and I need to stop thinking about the things Simon's mom said because I need to stop thinking about all of this. I'll mess everything up if I say anything because Simon seems happy the way we are. I think. And I have to stop questioning that or I'll mess everything up just by acting odd. So that's your advice, Fitz? Stop making things complicated and focus on taking care of your cats?"

She glanced down at the one sleeping on her lap. "Sorry, Henry. Fitz says I need to get up and trim your claws now."

****

The tree undecorating was one of the first events at the Christmas Festival. While there were several games aimed at kids, this one was reserved for adults, or at least almost adults. Competitors had to be sixteen or older. A smallish artificial tree was set up in the music room down the hall from most of the activity in the gym. It was adorned with three dozen plastic ornaments. On the floor next to the tree was a flat wooden box with the same number of compartments. Each competitor had to move all the ornaments from the tree to the squares in the box. To make it more difficult, the ornaments and squares were not all the same size. The larger ornaments didn't fit in the smaller squares, and each ornament had to fit inside a square to count as finished. The fastest time was declared the winner. Another difficulty was that competitors would be disqualified if any ornament hit the ground or if the tree toppled over. Several people had been disqualified in the previous years so the tree was looking rather rough as Tori and Eve pulled it out of the box.

"I think maybe we need a new tree next year," Eve said. A small tuft came off in her hand as she tried to fan out the branches.

"We could put an announcement in the bulletin to see if anyone wants to get rid of one after this year," Tori suggested.

Eve snorted. "Twenty of them would get dropped off. And only half would meet the size request."

"You're probably right." Figuring out what to do with nineteen extra trees didn't sound fun. Tori would let someone else worry about getting a new old tree while she focused on her current task. She started hanging the ornaments around the bottom before Eve had the top fanned out.

"Here's the box." Simon walked in carrying the flat box to collect the ornaments. It had been buried when they got out the other supplies so he told her he'd bring it to her when the stuff in front of it was out of the way.

Tori was expecting him, and yet she felt an odd sensation of surprise. Her fingers slipped on the string before she got the ornament in place.

"This good?" He set the box on the floor, and his eyes bounced between Tori and Eve for confirmation.

They both nodded. It was about five feet from the tree. They wanted people to have to move some without really running a race.

"And you have everything else you need?" He made sure he got nods from both of them again. Then he glanced around the room with some sort of mental checklist. "The two of you can run this by yourselves?"

"I think we could," Eve said. "But Ben will be here any minute to back us up."

Simon appeared slightly relieved. He paused for a few heartbeats of thought, then left in a rush.

Tori smiled to herself. She liked seeing him in charge. Somewhere in the back of her brain, she started humming his silly Christmas song while she continued to hang ornaments.

"Hi!" Eve's cheerful greeting made her look up to see Ben Shannon enter the room.

Tori and Ben exchanged greetings before he turned to Eve. "Were you *trying* to make me look bad?"

"What? Why do you say that?"

"I saw your mom in the hallway putting up signs to various events, and I asked her where the music room was."

Eve started laughing. Tori was confused.

"Why didn't you just say we were going to be in the room where we meet every Friday?"

"I don't know why I didn't say that," Eve said, "but I thought you knew..." She started pointing around the room. "There's a scale over there and a picture with rhythm patterns and there's a keyboard under that cover in the corner."

"Okay. In my defense, there could be anything under that cover in the corner."

Tori thought it was obviously keyboard-shaped, and he didn't mention any of the music-themed posters.

"And the guys are usually only in here a few minutes before we go across the hall."

Eve continued to eye him skeptically.

Rather than admit his defense was weak, Ben said, "What do you want me to do here?"

Eve turned to Tori for an opinion.

"I thought you could be the official scorekeeper while Eve and I handle the redecorating."

"Good idea," Eve said.

"That sounds like a respectable title," Ben said. "What exactly does the official scorekeeper do?"

Eve handed him a clipboard while Tori explained.

"You write down the name and address of all the contestants before they start, and then their times afterwards."

"Doesn't sound hard. Why do we need an address?"

"To mail the prize if the winner goes home before it's announced."

"What's the prize?"

"Pans and Plates gift card," Eve said. "Dan donated two. Do you know where you can win the other one?" She was asking Tori.

"I think Simon said that would be the stocking stuffer station."

Ben smiled. "Try to say that five times fast."

All three of them paused, clearly thinking the words but no one tried to say it out loud.

"Can I compete in this?" he asked.

Tori and Eve glanced at each other and shrugged. Tori said, "It might be good to have a practice run at resetting."

Eve nodded as well. "We'll time you now and then you'll be the time to beat."

"Great!" Ben set the clipboard aside and made sure he understood the rules. He hurried to get all the ornaments into the box while Eve timed him.

Tori and Eve timed themselves getting all the ornaments back on the tree.

"Should I write that down, too?" Ben asked jokingly.

"Actually, yeah," Eve said. "Just make a little note in the corner. We won't time ourselves every time, but maybe one more near the end, and we'll see how much faster we get with practice."

Tori smiled at the idea. They were going to get a lot of practice and competing with themselves might make it more fun.

Eve peered over Ben's shoulder. "Uh... you didn't write your last name or your address. What kind of official scorekeeper are you?"

"I apologize for not taking my duties seriously," Ben said very *un*seriously. Though he did add the information.

The game was all set with fifteen minutes to spare, and Tori suddenly felt like a third wheel as Ben and Eve gazed at each other a bit sappily. "I'm going to walk around to check on some other setup," she told them. "I'll be back in five minutes, and then if anyone's here, we'll go ahead and start early."

Eve said she liked the plan and Ben gave her a thumbs up. She suspected they both forgot about her the moment she left the room.

Tori peeked in another classroom where the sixth-graders were doing a last-minute rehearsal for their skit. She would have to miss that. In the gym, she saw a station for buying and frosting cookies and several games for little kids. One would have them reaching into gift bags to find numbers that matched prizes and another where they played shepherd by trying to line up sheep in a certain order. Tori walked past Matt setting up his DJ station. She overheard James trying to convince him not to start with The Chicken Dance.

Then she almost literally bumped into Simon.

"Are you looking for me?" he asked.

She shook her head, though she felt so happy to see him she wasn't entirely sure she was telling the truth. "I just wanted to stretch my legs a minute before we get started."

He seemed relieved. "Everyone is here who said they'd be here. I think it's actually going to run smoothly." He pointed towards the door. "We're even letting in some early guests who look eager."

"Wonderful. I better go run my station."

"Thank you!" Simon called after her.

Event excitement thrummed through her as Tori returned to the music room, smiling at a few people she passed. The room was not still as Mr. Donnelly was scrambling to undecorate the tree when she entered. He was nearly finished so she stayed by the doorway watching.

Eve called out a time that beat Ben's by twenty seconds.

"I guess there's a new sheriff in town," Mr. Donnelly said.

"I hoped my time would stand longer," Ben said, "but at least I lost to a worthy opponent."

Eve smirked at both of them. By the time she and Tori had the tree ready, the line had formed for the game. A rhythm quickly formed of decorating the tree and then catching her breath while it got undecorated. Ben kept good records and slipped a few ornaments on the tree whenever he had time. The game was only scheduled to last an hour, but they would keep going until everyone who got in line had a turn. Last year, that had taken twenty minutes extra.

Near the end of the hour was someone Tori recognized from somewhere other than church. It was Mr. Tanner's grandson. She had seen him in the hall before his turn and hoped they could get away with minimal small talk. It wasn't a good time.

"Hey, Tori, right?" He remembered her.

"Hi, um..." she only remembered he was related to Mr. Tanner, not his name.

"Nick," he supplied.

"I haven't seen you here before."

"Yeah, I'm not... A friend talked me into coming. Said there'd be free food, but I haven't seen anything free."

"Well, it's a fundraiser for the church," she said. "But donations make a lot of it cheap." She needed to keep the game moving. "Do you know how this works?"

"Yeah. Clipboard guy explained it to me."

Tori looked to Eve to see if she was ready to time him. She was giving Nick a suspicious look that was likely only partly fueled by him calling her boyfriend clipboard guy. The other part had to do with wondering how he knew Tori. Tori ignored the uncomfortable moment. "Ready?"

Eve nodded and said, "Go!"

Nick grabbed an ornament with each hand and had to let go of one when neither wanted to budge. He was moving quickly yet didn't appear to be trying hard. Then he knocked the tree over when he was about halfway done. "Ah! Am I the first to do that?"

"No," Tori assured him. "Good try."

He handed her the ornament he was holding. "I guess you have to put this back on now."

"Of course." She was confused because he sounded as though he was apologizing when it should be obvious that she'd signed up to put the ornaments on over and over. And she was having fun doing it.

"How much longer do you have to be here?" he asked.

"Until the line finishes," she said. "Then I have to clean up." She was already rehanging ornaments to reinforce the point that she didn't have time to talk. After he left, she realized that he might have been asking when she would have time to talk. She put him out of her head and smiled at the next competitor.

They stayed thirty minutes after the hour. Tori didn't mind because she was busy, but she was a little surprised people were willing to wait that long. Ben and Eve helped her take down the tree and get it pushed into a corner with the other supplies. Simon was going to use the room to lead something called Christmas Carol Name that Tune later. The three of them went to the gym together. Ben and Eve went to guess how many candy canes were stuffed into a big jar. Tori surveyed the organized chaos around her. She hadn't decided what to do next when Nick appeared at her elbow.

"Hello again," he said.

She smiled politely. She didn't know the guy so she had no reason to want to avoid him, but he gave the impression he'd been watching for her. That made her wary that this conversation would end with her saying she wasn't interested in exchanging numbers or something equally uncomfortable.

"My grandpa said you found a new job right away."

"Yeah. I hope he's enjoying his retirement."

Nick scoffed. "He's bored. I mean, he's determined to fill his time with a new hobby, but he's already abandoned knitting and photography. Last I heard, he planned to take up gardening. But it's December, so..."

"Indoor plants maybe?" Tori suggested.

"Huh? I didn't think of that." He tilted his head towards the sheep game. "What is going on over there?"

"Kids try to line up the sheep so they match the order on a set they can't see. It's all luck. They win a prize if they happen to guess right."

"They seem really excited about some trinket."

Tori didn't know the prize for that game, but she assumed the kids were excited because they were having fun trying. Sometimes it wasn't about the prize. She didn't feel like explaining that and was looking around the room for Simon. If one of his second shift volunteers didn't show up, they could rescue each other right now.

Matt came to her rescue instead because he announced at that moment that he was about to start a game of Matt Says.

"I'm gonna play," she told Nick. "I'll see you later." She began to move but discovered that he was moving the same way she was.

"What's Matt Says?" he asked.

"It's basically Simon Says, but with music and a DJ named Matt."

"Uh... okay." He took a spot next to her looking less than enthusiastic. Perhaps he'd get out early.

Simon knew what was coming when he recognized one of his songs. It used to be his song anyway. Matt had sped it up, stripped the lyrics and added a reverb fade over a steady bass beat. He put it on a loop and used it for Matt Says. Simon expected another round and he wasn't the only one. Several kids ran towards the dance floor before Matt announced he was getting ready to start.

Tori would want to play, especially after she missed the first round. Simon hadn't seen her yet though. Was she still stuck at the undecorating? He watched the dance floor fill up and spotted her. Good. She was finding time to enjoy the festival. She smiled at Matt and...

Who was that guy following her? He took a place next to her as though he belonged there. It appeared as though Tori was explaining the game to him. Was it possible he was some random dude who had managed to go his whole life without ever being introduced to Simon Says and just asked the first person he saw? It was possible but not likely. Did Tori know him?

Matt reminded everyone they'd be out if they did anything when he didn't say "Matt says." That guy didn't need Tori to explain it. Matt started everyone with some very simple dance moves, stepping side to side and clapping. He wore a headset microphone so he could demonstrate his instructions. Then he had everyone mirroring a disco point. The first time he didn't say "Matt says," he dropped into the worm. Most of the people watching laughed and two younger kids dropped to the floor and realized they were out.

The familiar sound of Tori's laugh reached Simon through the crowd. She wasn't laughing louder than anyone else. He just knew her laugh well. She said something to that guy next to her, probably about how she would have been out if Matt had said "Matt says" because she couldn't do that.

Matt said do a grapevine. He modeled it a few times and didn't call anyone out until they had a chance to learn it. He told them to add a funky head bob. The crowd looked silly, and they looked delighted to look silly together. Except for that guy. His moves were half-hearted at best and showed he was only participating to be near Tori.

When Matt said to stop without adding his name, that guy stopped. But he restarted when he realized his mistake. It looked as though Tori noticed but didn't say anything. Matt sent someone else off the floor and another young girl moved off on her own.

The game continued. Everything Matt said, he chanted with the music, and he primarily suggested rhythmic moves.

"Matt says step side to side again. Matt says clap three times." He clapped with his followers. "Now high five someone near you." He lifted his hand in an imaginary high five that turned into pointing at someone he caught moving with him.

That guy next to Tori had tried to slap her hand. She laughed and said something that probably had to do with him being out now. He shrugged and stayed next to her. What was he saying?

"Matt says march. Matt says keep marching and repeat after me. Merry Christmas. Incarnation rocks! Now freeze your feet." He scanned the room and didn't catch anyone who fell for it. "Matt says freeze your feet. Now Matt says raise the roof." He pumped his arms in the air.

Tori looked radiant as she copied him. She nodded at something that guy said without looking at him. It was hard to tell if she was brushing him off or just trying to focus on the game.

"Don't let your arms get tired," Matt said.

There was a strange ripple across the floor as many participants glanced at each other trying to figure out if they might be accidentally following an instruction they shouldn't. Matt cracked up. He laughed so hard he couldn't talk and had to put his arms down. Tori started laughing along with most of the people around her. She nodded encouragingly at a teenage girl in front of her who seemed to be concerned they might be out for laughing when Matt hadn't said to laugh.

That guy barely laughed, but he still put his arms down to wait for Matt to get control of the situation. Simon briefly wondered if he should turn the game into Simon Says. But Matt pulled himself together and resumed raising the roof. He said, "Matt says it's okay to laugh. I didn't mean to confuse anyone. Now put your arms down. Got you and you." He motioned a couple more off the floor. The crowd he'd started with was down to about a dozen.

"Matt says put your arms down," he said.

Tori shared a commiserating look with that guy next to her as she shook out her arms. He tried to appear sympathetic without acting as though *his* arms were tired, and they weren't because he'd already rested while everyone else kept playing along.

"Matt says take three steps to the left while - your left - while miming pulling a rope." He'd recognized possible confusion in the middle of his direction. "Matt says throw your hands up and yell, 'God bless us, every one, every one.'" After a pause for them to comply, he asked them to do it again.

That guy was the only one who put his hands up. They only went up part way and his mouth didn't open. It might have looked as though he caught himself if Simon hadn't been watching him do all the moves with so little enthusiasm. Matt noticed though.

"You're out." He pointed and motioned him off the floor.

That guy finally walked away. Tori glanced after him. Was she also thinking it was about time, or was she checking to see which way he went?

Matt continued his chanting instructions, including a few that got more laughs, until he whittled his competition down to three. "Okay, game's over," he said. "These are our winners. Come up to claim your prizes."

Tori had lasted until the end. She slapped hands with the other winners as they walked towards Matt. She spoke to him briefly, probably to thank him for making the game fun, before she accepted a ticket that could be used for one of the activities around the gym. And then she walked straight to Simon. She must have known he was watching.

"I'm going to use my ticket to get a cookie," she said. "I think I earned it. Why didn't you play with us?"

She meant everyone who played when she said us. Simon knew that, and yet he couldn't help wondering if she also meant her and that guy who followed her.

"It was fun to watch," he said.

"You just knew I'd beat you," she teased.

"Who was that guy next to you?" Simon winced internally at the question he hadn't intended to ask and the accusing tone he especially hadn't intended to use. He knew the guy wasn't anyone Tori knew well. Curiosity still pushed the question out.

"Nick Tanner. Or actually I don't..." She tipped her eyes towards the ceiling for information that wasn't there. "He's Mr. Tanner's grandson, but I don't remember if he said that was his last name."

"What's he doing here?"

"Someone told him there was free food, I guess." She shrugged.

Simon kicked himself both for asking another question about that guy and for his rather uncharitable attitude towards him. He wasn't unwelcome just because he wasn't a parishioner. Simon did wonder why he wasn't with whomever invited him though.

"I think he's near our age, maybe a bit older," Tori said. "We might know who he knows." Her eyes scanned the gym. Was she looking for him? Simon was annoyed because he knew it was his fault they were even still talking about that guy. "He was cheating, you know."

"What?" She resumed eye contact.

"At Matt Says. He should have been out at least twice before he actually left."

"Oh, I did suggest he was out once, but he said he only had to leave if Matt caught him. Some people do play that way so..."

"That's not how you were playing just now. He didn't notice other people walking off whether Matt told them to or not?"

"I don't really know what he noticed or didn't."

"Even pretty young kids could tell there was an honor system going on," Simon said.

"Honor system?" Tori narrowed her eyes. "That sounds..."

Simon interrupted before she thought of a way to finish. "He who is dishonest in little things is dishonest in big things."

"That's true, but... Did you want me to escort him off the floor or otherwise make a big deal in the middle of a game?" She was eyeing him as though she didn't understand why *he* was making a big deal about it.

Simon tried to dial back his overreaction. "No. Of course not. But you could have pointed out the rules other people were following."

"I just didn't think it mattered," she said.

"It doesn't matter."

"Then what do you want from me?"

"I want you to marry me so I never have to worry about whether another guy matters." That wasn't entirely true. He wanted her to *want* to marry him. But he shouldn't have said that either because Tori appeared to be deciding between surprise and confusion and he saw more anger than both.

"I can't believe you just said that," she snapped.

"Neither can I." It was not the right time or place for a serious discussion.

"Simon!" Eve called his name from nearby. Before he could react, she was tugging on his arm. "Everyone is waiting for you to play Name That Christmas Tune."

He checked the time. He was late. But Tori was more important. He needed to arrange a time to talk, and he'd do it right there if she wanted.

"Go." Tori shooed him as though he couldn't get out of her sight fast enough.

"Come on." Eve was still tugging his arm.

Simon allowed himself to be pulled away from Tori. Eve let go as soon as he started moving.

"I can't believe you're late," she said. "Mom's been telling everyone how perfectly you've handled the event. What's she gonna say when she finds out about this disaster?"

Starting a game a few minutes late hardly qualified as a disaster. Simon still hoped his mom didn't hear about it because he had a terrible feeling that she would know - somehow - that it had something to do with Tori. Thinking about what his mom thought about Tori had already gotten him into too much trouble.

****

A cookie with one bite missing sat on a napkin in Tori's hand. She'd used her ticket for one because she said she was going to. She took a bite because the woman at the station seemed to be watching to see if she enjoyed it. After giving the woman a thumbs up, Tori moved away from the table and didn't have the appetite to finish. She saw Nick with a guy who seemed familiar but not enough to know if she'd seen him at church or somewhere else around town. They were in line for pizza.

Tori positioned herself behind them with some crowd cover between. Then she scanned for an exit strategy. Joseph and Emily Zeibert had their kids by the sheep game. It would be hard to talk over the music, but she could ask Matt if he'd gotten any unusual requests. A few other familiar people were scattered about. If Nick approached her again, she could at least make sure she wasn't alone.

Nick and his friend got their pizza and immediately moved towards the door. Neither appeared to be looking around for anyone. As they disappeared, Tori realized it wasn't only Nick she wanted to avoid. She was relieved that she hadn't had to engage any of her friends. She needed time to herself, time to parse the crazy thoughts in her head.

What were Simon's exact words? I want you to marry me so I don't have to wonder if another guy matters? Or did he say worry? She'd thought he was joking. Tori had been struggling to admit the depth of her feelings for Simon and to control her wish that he could feel the same. The idea that he would make light of something tying her up in knots had produced a visceral anger. It had been difficult to think straight. As a result, she had failed to think straight.

After a minute to calm down - and another bite of sweet cookie helped - she didn't believe Simon would joke like that. In fact, she knew he hadn't been joking. But how sincere was he? Even if he did have romantic interest in her, he wouldn't jump straight to let's get married, would he? It was true that they'd been friends so long that they didn't need time to get to know each other, and most of the thoughts Tori had been trying not to think about Simon involved starting a family together and building one life out of two, not sharing pizza like they'd done many times before.

Tori was beginning to admit to herself that she wanted to marry Simon. She wasn't ready to admit that to him. Her head didn't fit around the possibility of Simon thinking anything similar, much less blurting it out. What had he meant then? Maybe he was only wishing their relationship was different without really wanting that.

They both knew they might be standing in each other's way when it came to romantic prospects. Hadn't Tori just been hoping that talking to Simon would discourage Nick from talking to her? Had other guys been similarly discouraged without her knowledge? Certainly women had assumed Simon was unavailable because of her. She knew a few in college who would have tried to spend more time with him if they'd believed her when she said they were only friends.

Maybe that's what Simon meant, that he worried about getting in the way of Tori meeting the guy who could be her future groom. Maybe he meant it would be convenient if they wanted to marry each other rather than having to find others. Tori thought that was a reasonable explanation. But she didn't like it.

"You look lost."

Tori jumped as Emily addressed her.

"Sorry," Emily said. "I didn't mean to startle you." The baby in her arms was staring at Tori with his mouth hanging open, unnervingly focused.

Tori was embarrassed to realize she likely had a similar expression as Emily approached. She snapped herself out of the stupor and forced a smile. "Hi. Just got caught in a daze for a second. Are your kids having fun?"

Emily smiled brightly. "I think so. They wanted to do the sheep guessing game, and Joseph just got them in line for a third try. His competitive streak might not let them walk away until someone wins."

Tori followed Emily's gaze and spotted Joseph with the two older kids. He was gesturing with both hands and appeared to be strategizing their next guesses.

"He's trying to figure out the angle," Emily said. She continued in response to Tori's confusion. "He actually calculated the odds of matching the four numbers at random and thinks too many kids are winning for it to really be random."

"That's... kind of... intense." Tori hoped she'd picked an inoffensive word to say she couldn't believe how much effort he'd put into winning his kids a rubber duck with a Santa hat.

"Merry Christmas!" Jackson and Cassidy – also from the young adult group – joined them. The couple spoke in unison and then gave each other a sideways glance as though giving the blame for the unintended cuteness.

Tori smiled and Emily said, "Merry Christmas to you, too."

"Congrats on the Simon Says win, Tori," Cassidy said.

"It's Matt Says, which is much cooler," Emily said. She focused on Tori. "No offense to anyone named Simon. I just meant the rather dull way the game is usually played."

"I know," she said. "Matt's a natural entertainer. And thank you." Tori nodded graciously to Cassidy. "It was a hard-fought victory."

"If you knew you could put that on your resume," Jackson said, "you probably would have gotten snatched up before my dad could hire you."

Tori pretended to wipe her forehead in relief as they all smiled at the silly banter. James popped up and mumbled an apology to the others before he addressed Tori. "Where's Simon?"

"He's doing the guess the carol thing."

"Oh, right." James seemed unsure what to do with that news.

"Is there a problem?" Tori asked.

"A bunch of people are asking for another round of Matt Says so he wants to know if he can do it earlier than planned."

She glanced around for opinions. Cassidy shrugged. Emily said, "I don't see how that would hurt anything."

Jackson grinned and said, "I'll play."

James eyes Tori hopefully. "So if we go ahead, I can tell Simon or mom or whoever asks that you said it was okay?"

It was flattering that James thought her word carried so much weight. Flattering and a bit unsettling. She wasn't as well-known at the church as Mrs. Donnelly. If James or Matt used her name to justify their decision to someone outside the family, the response might be "Who's that?" Tori shrugged as she nodded to James, trying not to think that a lot of people at the church would answer that question with "Simon's girlfriend" or even "Simon's wife." She was still trying to accept that those assumptions didn't bother her because they were wrong but because part of her had always wished they weren't.

"My mother-in-law is here somewhere," Emily said. "I'm going to find her to hold the baby so I can play, too." Her eyes zeroed in on the older Mrs. Ziebart before she finished the sentence about finding her, and she darted off in that direction.

"Who else wants to give her some competition?" Jackson glanced between Cassiday and Tori with a challenge in his eyes.

"I'm in," Cassidy said.

"I already have a trophy." Tori held up her half-eaten cookie. "I should let someone else have a chance."

Jackson grinned at her fake bragging and ushered Cassidy towards the dance floor. There was a pause in the music as Matt made an announcement. "Great news, everyone. Another round of Matt Says will begin right after this song for all the great-grandparents here. I've heard this guy was called the singing cowboy."

What sounded like a pretty old rendition of Rudolph started playing. Tori didn't recognize it, but she noticed Mr. Donnelly frowning at Matt, which made her wonder if the song wasn't quite as old as he implied. It was entertaining to watch a crowd form around the edges of the dance floor. Kids found places right in front of the DJ table but adults merely hovered, ready to play but making sure no one expected them to dance to an old cowboy song. There were more adults in this round than the one Tori played. She liked to think she'd inspired at least a few of them to have a little fun, though it was more likely Matt's goofy leadership that brought them into the game.

Tori didn't even watch half the game before she grew restless. She worried that someone would engage her in conversation as soon as it was over. Her thoughts were swirling around Simon and marriage and insisting she stop trying to push those thoughts away. She wanted to be alone before she churned up enough emotion to start crying out of nowhere. But her legs didn't carry her outside where she could actually be alone. They carried her to the hallway outside the room Name that Christmas Tune was happening. She stood against the wall and listened closely for Simon's voice.

Simon had the keyboard set to synthesize an organ. Three notes resounded into the hallway before he asked Team B to make a guess. Tori didn't recognize the song, but it was obviously not *Silent Night.* She knew Simon was scoffing at that guess on the inside, though no trace of it was in his voice when he said it was wrong and moved to Team C. Simon awarded a point for *God Rest Ye Merry Gentlemen* before he started another song with only one note.

He kept the game moving, and Tori didn't try to keep up. She listened to his voice without hearing the words. Every phrase triggered pictures of him showing up to mow her lawn, singing with her while decorating the trees at church, waiting patiently on the other end of the phone for her to stop crying the day it hit her that her mom was actually living in a different state. She thought of him supporting her in her job search and teasing her when she referred to her cats as gentlemen.

Tori remembered Simon's mom suggesting that he wanted a sign that a romantic shift would be welcome. And then the memories in her head became related, one after another she saw times when someone asked if she was dating Simon, and she insisted there was friendship between them and only friendship, that there would only ever be friendship. Her mind replayed times she told Simon how annoyed she was that people kept asking. All together, the defensiveness behind her memories was crystal clear to her. Tori was so afraid that Simon didn't want more that she always shut down the topic before there could be any hint of a reaction from him.

It would be impossible for him to admit stronger feelings when she appeared adamantly against the idea. But that didn't actually mean she was stopping him from something he wanted. He could be perfectly happy avoiding the subject. How could she find out if he wanted to make a change without finding out that he didn't? How would she ask him about their relationship without jeopardizing the relationship? Tori had never wanted to talk to Simon more. Or less.

Laughter burst out of the room near her and brought her attention to the present.

"That's not a Christmas song," someone said.

A bit more ribbing had Tori guessing that someone had guessed *Bingo*. She smiled to herself as Simon got the room back in order.

"We're up to six notes," he said. "Surely someone will get it this time."

The notes were familiar. Tori felt the lyrics would come to her if she heard it one more time. Maybe she'd know if she'd listened when he played five notes. Simon called on Team C, and someone guessed *Away in a Manger*. Tori shook her head. She still couldn't place the song, but she knew that wasn't it.

"No," Simon said. "Team A?"

There was a pause while Tori assumed team members were whispering about what to guess. "Is it... *The Snow Lay on the Ground*?"

"Great job. That makes A and B tied now."

Tori nodded to herself. She could hear the lyrics now, or at least some of them. That wasn't a common one. She expected Simon to give them an easy one next. But she didn't stay to listen more. She needed to be alone. On her way to her car, she texted Simon that she'd be back in time to help with cleanup in case he was looking for her before that.

****

"Have you seen Tori?"

Simon was sweeping up colorful sprinkles from the floor when his sister approached with the question. "She went home," he said without looking up. "She said she'd be back to help us clean up."

"She went home?" There was a note of disbelief in Eve's voice. "Is she feeling okay?"

"I doubt she'd be planning to come back if she was sick." Simon still didn't look at Eve as he spoke because he thought he'd see suspicion in her eyes. But he was also keeping his eyes on the broom to keep from tripping any of the kids who kept walking by as though they were oblivious to what he was doing. Some of the sprinkles were going to have to wait for the more thorough cleanup later. He got the bulk of the spill into the dustpan and then the trash.

"Thanks, Simon." The woman running the cookie decorating station spared him a moment of gratitude in between making sure all the other sprinkle tops stayed in place.

Eve hadn't left. "When did Tori leave?" she asked.

"She texted me about a half hour ago."

"You didn't talk to her?" That was either suspicion or indignation, neither of which was called for.

"I was in the middle of the Christmas carol game."

Eve raised her eyebrows as though she was expecting more explanation.

Simon had nothing else to say. He'd been worried since Tori left - or at least since he found out she left - that it was his fault. He couldn't stop to think about that in the middle of the Christmas Festival.

"I thought she planned to stay the whole time," Eve said.

Tori had planned to stay the whole time. Simon did not confirm that to his sister because that would only lead to questions about why she changed her mind, questions he couldn't answer and didn't have time to think about. "You'll have to ask her why she went home because I don't know," he said. "Do you want to put this broom away for me?"

She laughed, but she continued to eye him speculatively for a few moments before she walked away.

Simon shrugged her off as he returned the broom and dustpan to a closet. He paused at the doorway before going into the gym. Matt was doing a good job with the music volume. It was faintly recognizable and not blaring from the opposite end. There was a murmur of crowd noise punctuated by short laughs and louder exclamations. Nothing appeared to be on fire, metaphorically speaking, as volunteers were in all the places he checked and none of them were trying to flag him down.

He spotted his mom chatting with a few people by a game where kids tried to guess which candy cane was tied to a star. She was calm and the people talking to her were calm so he could assume they weren't asking her to address anything literally on fire. He moved towards another game to watch. Someone had created a maze on the floor with red masking tape. One person (with a helper if that person was very young) sat on each side of the square and pulled a string to get the wise men attached to move towards him. They had to work together to get the magi from the start to the baby Jesus at the end.

The maze itself was simple. Simon navigated it with his eyes in a few seconds. But getting everyone to pull the string just right was causing a lot of shouting and cajoling. He watched a second group accomplish the task faster than the first before he moved to the side and saw Fr. John approaching.

"Hey, Simon. I want to thank you again for all you did to pull this off without a hitch."

"I had a lot of help," Simon said, "and a great template from previous years."

Fr. John nodded. "Still, the ladies at the ticket table tell me we're on pace to set a record."

"That's great." Simon couldn't take credit for the excellent turnout, but he knew the priest was sincere with his appreciation so he didn't try any harder to deflect it.

"Have you tried any of the games? I think you made a good call on that sheep game." He winked. "I've heard a few comments on the odds."

Simon was going to say he intended to try the wreath toss. Aside from the tree undecorating, it was probably the only game not aimed specifically at kids. Before he could open his mouth, they were joined by another man. It was clear he was more interested in talking to the priest. Simon wished them both a merry Christmas as he slipped away.

The wreath toss had paper plates with the centers cut out, decorated to resemble wreaths by one of the elementary classes. The object was to toss them frisbee-style through the windows of a big cardboard house. James and a couple of his friends were manning it.

"We should probably let Simon stand at the kid line," he said.

One of his friends laughed but cut it off quickly. The other kept a straight face.

Simon probably shouldn't have, but he enjoyed the fact that they seemed afraid to mess with him. He took his wreaths to the adult line without responding to his brother's jest. One of his plate wreaths bounced off the edge of the window. The other two - and he only needed two to win - sailed through cleanly. James held up a box for him to take a little candy cane. He pocketed the treat thinking that he'd give it to Tori, though he couldn't do that while she wasn't there.

As someone else began a turn tossing, Simon heard his mom's voice at his elbow. "Have you seen Tori?"

"She went home," he said, turning to face her. "She said she'd be back for cleanup."

Her eyes searched his face, possibly trying to find the reason for Tori's absence. She might have seen some guilt because she said, "What did you do?"

"I didn't do anything," he said.

"Maybe that's the problem." His mom lowered her glasses and peered at him over the frames.

"Really, mom? You're doing the glasses thing with me?"

"Was there something you should have done? Like maybe listen to your mother?"

Simon said nothing and let her stare at him silently lifting her eyebrows as she drove her point home. He was afraid that listening to her was part of the problem, and that wasn't an argument he was going to make out loud.

She pushed her glasses up when she was satisfied with her intimidation. "For now, you can probably tell Tori she doesn't need to bother coming back if she's not up to it for any reason." She cleared her throat to pointedly fill in some blame. "She's not on the official sign-up so no one will miss her, and we have plenty of help."

"I might do that," he said. While he needed to talk to her, he couldn't really do that surrounded by other people.

"And I might see if I can get a few bodies for putting away the church decorations." His mom smiled somewhat wickedly before turning away.

Simon moved to a relatively quiet corner to text Tori. He let her know they had enough volunteers for the cleanup without her if she wanted to stay home. She responded immediately, saying she'd see him at church the next day.

See him at church? The answer stung. It was as though she wanted to pretend she wasn't mad at him for suggesting they get married. The strong emotion he'd seen in her eyes needed to be addressed. If they just swept that under the rug without talking about it, their friendship wasn't as solid as they thought it was. He asked if he could call her when he got home. She agreed with a very bland "ok."

The event would be winding down soon. Simon spent the last bit of it looking for things he could box up or put away early to speed up everyone getting home. More people than expected stayed for the final shift, and Simon ended up leaving about the time the cleanup was scheduled to end, which he considered early. When he got home, he picked up a Bible. At some point in his childhood, he'd started holding a Bible whenever he had a specific request from God. Somone had told him God speaks to us through his word, and Simon liked to hold it when he spoke back. It was because it felt juvenile that he still did it. He was still a child in God's eyes.

Simon asked God to guide his words as he spoke to Tori. He'd been certain he couldn't continue the relationship as it was, that it was too painful to have her see him as a friend when he wanted more. And then he was certain he had to continue for her sake. Now he was admitting he didn't know what to do or even really what Tori wanted him to do. He needed to ask if she had stronger feelings for him that she was hiding from others. He needed the answer even if he didn't like it. And then he needed to assure both of them that he wasn't going anywhere no matter what.

He set down the Bible and picked up his phone. It took three very long rings for her to answer.

"Hey, Simon. Are you home already?"

"Yeah. Everything finished smoothly."

"Great. Sorry I didn't help."

"You did help. A lot," he said. "I heard several people say how fun the undecorating was."

"It was fun for me, too."

The conversation was stilted and forced. Despite the prayer, Simon didn't know how to get Tori to tell him what she needed from him. "How are you?" he asked.

"Uh... I'm ... okay?" It sounded as though she couldn't tell if he wanted an answer.

His question had come out like one of those greetings that aren't real questions. "I mean, really how are you? Eve was afraid you might have left early because you were sick."

"Oh, no. I'm fine."

"And I was afraid you left early because you were ticked off at me."

Tori said nothing, but he could almost hear her uncertainty. She wanted to say something.

He wanted to know what she was holding back. "I'm sorry for upsetting you," he said. "I'd like to blame my mom for what I said, but I don't think it'll help to bring her into this."

"How is it your mom's fault?"

"She's been badgering me about... you."

Tori made a sound that might've been a laugh.

"Was that a laugh?" he asked.

"A little. I... she said something to me, too."

"What did she say to you?"

"I think you should tell me what she's badgering you about first."

Simon almost smiled. Tori had relaxed and was being difficult on purpose rather than trying to hide something. Bringing his mom into the conversation had apparently helped after all. He was going to run with it. "She cornered me with the crazy idea that I should give you an engagement ring for Christmas. Then she kept bringing it up. She even tried to tell me afterward that you were disappointed. But you liked the song, right?"

"Uh, yeah." Her voice was off somehow.

"You're not just trying to let me off the hook, right? You really liked it?"

"Yeah. It was really one of my favorite presents this year."

"And... just to prove me right for the sake of argument... if, or maybe when, you find yourself in a position where you expect to get engaged, you wouldn't want the ring for Christmas, right? Wouldn't you rather it was something separate and not in front of... people?"

"I, um... I don't... Probably. It's hard to say with... uh, so many hypotheticals."

She seemed to have trouble picturing herself getting engaged to some random guy. That was somewhat comforting. It didn't get him closer to knowing if she could picture him. "What did my mom say to you?" he asked.

"Oh, uh... she seems convinced that..." Tori sucked in a breath and continued with warp speed words. "She thinks you're madly in love with me and just waiting for permission to admit it. I thought she was the only person content to leave us alone so I... I almost laughed, like, that's everyone now."

"That made you laugh? You usually get mad whenever anyone says anything about us being more than friends." *Including me*, he thought.

"I guess it depends on how it's... or maybe who. I know your mom loves you and was trying to help. Most people are just looking for gossip."

"How it's brought up," he repeated. This felt like the band-aid moment. "Is there a way I could bring it up that wouldn't make you mad?"

"What do you mean?"

Simon needed to rip harder. "Us being more than friends. When I said something today, you were really mad, like almost literal sparks coming out of your eyes. Did I just do it again or is this something we can actually talk about?"

"We can... talk." Her tone was hesitant but not angry. That was encouraging.

"Why did you get so angry? It's not a new idea. Haven't you ever thought about it?"

"Yeah. I... of course. I think your entire family and my sister, too, thought we were secretly dating when we first came back from school. It'd be impossible not to... but I... It was the way you said it so casually. I thought you were joking, that... something in the moment made me feel like you were laughing about the idea of marrying me. And already it sounds stupid to get so offended because I know you wouldn't... I think maybe I'm detoxing from all the sugar I had in Florida."

"I wasn't joking," he said.

"I know. As soon as I calmed down, I realized you meant it'd be convenient if things were different between us and... and then neither of us would have to worry about trying to find someone else, especially someone who wouldn't mind us being friends."

"That's not... I don't think it would be *convenient*."

Tori was quiet a moment, thinking. "Simon... do you..." In the stretching silence, he sensed that she was struggling to ask something important, that it was time to say something important.

"I *am* madly in love with you and maybe done waiting for permission to say it. But it doesn't have to change anything. I know you've adopted my family, and I won't make that awkward. I don't expect anything from you. I just... I want you to know that if you ever do want things to change between us, I'll be ready."

More silence, possibly the stunned variety rather than tongue-tied.

"Do you want time to think about that?" he asked.

"Yes, I... I..."

Simon didn't know if not pressing her now was really for her sake, or if he was simply afraid she'd say something he didn't want to hear. But he was ready to hang up either way. "I'll let you go then and see you at church tomorrow."

"Uh... good night, Simon."

He put down the phone and immediately regretted letting her go. He wasn't in a better position than before he talked to her. He knew she was no longer angry about what he said at the festival, but he didn't know if she was angry about the declaration she might not have wanted to hear. He said it wouldn't be awkward with his family, but he couldn't actually control that. If Tori felt weird about hanging around him and his family now, then she felt weird.

The impulse to call her back made him reach for the phone before he restrained his arm. The ball was in her court. Demanding she toss it back was a bad idea. He told her nothing needed to change. He had to continue as though nothing had in order to keep his word.

It was still dark. Tori wasn't entirely sure she'd fallen asleep, but there hadn't been a cat kneading and purring by her ear a second ago. Maybe she'd been out? She rolled over to look at her clock. It had been a few hours, and the alarm would beep soon. She closed her eyes, enjoying the way the fogginess of sleep dulled her emotions.

Beeping from the alarm woke her again. Tori reached out an arm to shut it off. She switched on a light that burned her eyes to tiny slits. Hard to go back to sleep like that anyway. When she could see, she sat up and looked back at Fitz sleeping near her pillow. He picked his head up slightly but put it back down when she got out of bed without petting him.

She went to the sink in the bathroom and splashed cold water on her face. And then she froze with the faucet running and water dripping down both her forearms. Was that a dream, or had she really texted Simon in the middle of the night to say she loved him? It felt real. Was it?

Tori shook off her stupor and turned off the water. She dried her hands and opened the drawer on her nightstand to retrieve her phone. Not only had she sent the message, Simon had replied with a thumbs up. She stared at it with a mix of disbelief and... well, annoyance. He'd been articulate and romantic on the phone when he told her he was in love with her. And now, after she spent hours of lost sleep pondering how to respond, kicking herself for being too shocked to say anything at the time, pinching herself that he'd said something so wonderful, wondering how it would feel to see him after admitting she felt the same way... now all she got was a thumbs up?

She scrambled a few eggs for breakfast. She watched them cook while scenes that still confused her and words that didn't feel real played in her head. How had she become so afraid she couldn't see what was obvious to Simon's mother? Had the fear been obvious, too? How had Simon just casually stated that he was madly in love with her? Despite the evidence on her phone, part of her was afraid she was going to find out that hadn't actually happened. It did happen though. And in the moment, she'd given him nothing but stunned silence. Perhaps a thumbs up wasn't the worst response.

The eggs were dry and even browned in spots before she refocused on her task. Tori ate them anyway and finished getting ready for church. She was consumed with questions about what happened next. Would she feel strange around Simon while they got used to the new reality? Would it affect their relationship in ways she couldn't predict? Who should she tell first?

A grin popped onto Tori's face as she pictured some reactions. Her mom would be calm, offering congratulations while insisting she knew it would happen eventually. Eve would probably demand to know how long they'd been hiding it. She turned up a happy song in her car and sang along, oblivious to the dirty snow on the edge of the road or how many of the houses had already taken down their Christmas decorations.

Tori entered the quiet church. Her eyes moved first to her typical pew. Simon and Grandpa Will weren't there yet. Then she looked at the decorations as she walked forward, remembering Simon helping her with the trees. She slipped into the center of the pew, leaving room for two next to her. Her brain failed to focus on any particular prayer or even coherent words. Her heart simply buzzed with gratitude for the first day of something new and wonderful.

Footsteps told her they were coming before she sensed the men next to her. She glanced at Grandpa Will as he sat and whispered, "You're late."

He sighed as though he deserved the accusation.

Simon nodded a greeting at her exactly as he always did. It surprised Tori with how normal it felt. Maybe, if she hadn't told him she loved him, too, he could've continued with their friendship just as it was. Maybe she didn't need to waste time on what ifs. And maybe she was a moron for expecting anything drastically different about walking into church.

She smiled again. It seemed Tori was so happy that even calling herself a moron made her smile, a pathetic assessment that pushed her smile even wider.

The congregation sang *The First Noel* and later the less common tune for *Away in a Manger*. Tori knew that Simon preferred that version, and she sang a little quieter to better hear him enjoying it. Tori walked out behind Simon and Grandpa Will, but she only made it halfway out the church before a woman jumped in her path.

"Tori, right?"

"Yeah, uh... hi." Tori stopped herself before she added Alexandra. She thought this woman was one of her sister's friends from high school. She was ten years older, maybe thirty pounds heavier and had brown hair instead of blonde. Tori wasn't entirely sure of her identity.

"It's Alexandra," the woman confirmed. "Is your sister here?"

"No, Liz moved to Florida a few years ago."

She nodded. "I'm still in Michigan. I'm just home visiting my parents for Christmas." Alexandra pointedly moved her eyes down the aisle and back. "Was that Simon Donnelly you were sitting with?"

"Yeah." Tori tried to answer casually, but she could tell another smile gave away that they were more than sitting together.

Alexandra gave a low whistle of approval and said, "Nice catch."

Tori redirected the conversation to small talk and left with a few updates to share with her sister. They still kept in touch online so Liz might already know her old friend's job and fiancé's name, but it would still be nice to share that she'd seen Alexandra in person.

The delay meant Tori arrived last to the Donnellys' house. Even Grandpa Will and his slow pace had made it inside. She wasn't nervous or even thinking about anyone's reaction if the new direction became obvious. She was only thinking of getting out of the cold.

She hadn't reached the first step when Simon opened the back door. He came through it rather than holding it for her, and she was about to ask if he left something in his car. He didn't go to his car. He moved straight to Tori and kissed her. He kissed her lips before she had time to appreciate what was about to happen, and it was over before she appreciated what was happening. Then he locked eyes with her to seek her opinion.

Her brain repeated "nice catch" and her mouth moved towards his in answer. The second kiss was long enough to fully register the new and wonderful Tori expected.

Simon took a step back and said, "There's a crowd in there. Can we stay out here?"

"It's cold out here," she said.

"I hadn't noticed."

He'd notice soon enough. Even though he'd lit a fire within her core, her fingers and toes were still approaching freezing.

"So I don't mess up again, when *is* the appropriate time to talk about us getting married?"

She laughed. "I don't know. I just know you don't start with marriage."

"We didn't start there."

He was right. Tori studied his very familiar face and knew they were a long way from where they started. She knew the shape of his eyes and the shape of his jaw. And when she shivered, she recognized the concern that appeared in his expression.

"Call me when you get home this afternoon," he said, taking her cold hand in his warm one to pull her inside.

"Okay." She closed the door solidly before she took off her coat, wondering if she'd agreed to talk about getting married or to talk about when they could talk about getting married. Her eyes danced against the smile she tried to hide while thinking about talking to Simon about whether they were talking about getting married or talking about talking about getting married. She almost laughed out loud as her mind went back to check to see if she'd gotten the thought straight. Maybe this was what people meant by the phrase deliriously happy.

Tori took one last glance at Simon - who appeared content to watch her have crazy thoughts - before she forced herself to take in her surroundings. A baby was crying. John must be there with his family. They stayed home most Sundays. She stepped into the kitchen and saw Ben, who must have come with Eve. Drew was still home from college. It *was* a fuller crowd than usual. Grandpa Will was already seated at the table with Simon's dad. James and Drew were claiming chairs and Matt was trying to put the two-year-old in his high chair backwards.

"Why isn't this working?" he asked playfully. Spencer only laughed and offered no help.

Matt flipped him over and tried to put him in sideways.

Tori smiled at the two of them as she approached Mrs. Donnelly taking a large casserole dish out of the oven. "Am I too late to help?"

Simon's mom shook her head. As soon as she had a free hand, she pointed at the glass bowl on the counter. "Take the fruit in and have everyone start passing that around."

"Got it." Tori took the bowl and held it next to Grandpa Will first. Once he had a scoop, she gave it to Simon.

"Why does Simon always get the food first just because he sits next to Grandpa?" James asked. It didn't sound as though he wanted an answer, just to complain about it.

"Does it matter?" Simon asked. "We're all going to eat at the same time."

"It used to matter," Eve said. "You used to pick out all the blueberries."

"Only after you picked out all the bananas."

"Just make sure Matt gets it last."

Matt huffed defensively. "I didn't know you hadn't eaten yet."

Tori had made her way to her usual seat next to Eve during the banter. Eve leaned over to explain. "Mom made chili last night. It's one of Drew's favorites. I warmed some up when I got home from work, then Matt polished off what was left even though he'd already had dinner. Drew came home a few minutes later - he'd been visiting his girlfriend - and was upset the chili was all gone before he had any."

"In Matt's defense," James said, "we all assumed Drew was late because he stopped somewhere for dinner."

"Mom told me there would be chili waiting for me."

"Well, in *my* defense..." Mrs. Donnelly set the meat and egg dish in front of her dad to start passing that around as well. "I made more than usual to make sure we'd have leftovers."

"This casserole reminds me of the bedroom carpet in that house your mom and I moved into when you were in college." Grandpa Will returned the spatula to the pan. "Do you remember that?"

"I remember... the house." Mrs. Donnelly glanced around the table, sharing amused looks regarding this random remark.

"That must have been some ugly carpet," Simon's dad said, then he winced apologetically. "Uh, no offense to this dish that is *supposed* to look like scrambled food."

There were a few chuckles at his qualification.

Tori thought the casserole looked and smelled delicious. After everyone had some and they said a prayer, she was able to confirm that it also tasted delicious. Drew talked about the classes he'd start in January, his last semester. Anna shared a few cute things Spencer had said recently. He was learning new words every day and even putting a few together. Grandpa Will was "reminded" of a few entertaining stories as well.

The lunch ended with the oldest and youngest people needing to go home for naps. Simon escorted his grandpa to the door, both of them assuring everyone they'd see or talk to them soon. Simon looked at Tori in the midst of saying goodbye to his family. She saw something special in his gaze, something that repeated the love he'd said to her. Was that new? Had he let his guard down after admitting how he felt, or had she been too afraid to look for it before?

"Help me pick a game, Tori." Eve was suddenly in her face and urging her to follow.

Tori went with Eve to a closet down the hall. It was lined with shelves full of board games. Eve opened the door to display the choices, but she was looking at Tori and not the games.

"Are you just waiting for me to suggest something?"

"Oh..." Eve bit the side of her lip and appeared to be hesitating to say something.

That was when it because obvious to Tori that she'd been called over not just to choose a game but for a private word. "Are you trying to tell me something or ask me something?" she said.

Eve smiled at what she interpreted as permission to plunge ahead. "I was worried when you left early yesterday. You and Simon seem okay though. Are you okay?"

"Yeah."

"Are you sure? When I asked him where you were, he looked... guilty and... not good."

"There was a little misunderstanding," Tori admitted. "But we talked it out." Because she'd already started grinning like a cheshire cat, she added an eyebrow wiggle to hint at how well it had been worked out.

Eve gasped. "Are you saying... Are you actually telling me that you guys are not *just* friends?"

Tori nodded. And she kept grinning. It was harder to stop now that Eve was mirroring it.

"Who else knows?" Eve glanced over her shoulder, presumably to ensure they were not being overheard.

"Um... well, I haven't told anyone else." Tori wasn't sure that meant no one else knew. She was starting to feel as though a lot of people knew before she did.

"Great! I'm gonna enjoy watching other people find out."

"Get the poker chips!" James' voice called.

Eve's expression shifted from excitement to a question. "Should we humor them or get my mom to do a separate girls' game?"

Tori shrugged. She was predisposed to enjoying anything at the moment.

"Poker it is." Eve grabbed the box of chips, then lowered her voice to remind Tori that Drew always bluffed and Matt couldn't keep a straight face.

A few hands into the game, Simon returned. Since he moved out, he had come back only rarely after driving Grandpa Will. Eve winked at Tori as though she knew exactly why he came back. He wanted to get opinions on some song lyrics, asked if grace and place was too obvious a rhyme and if calm meant the same as still to anyone.

Several people gave opinions to which he nodded gratefully. Then Drew sarcastically thanked him for interrupting the game before inviting him to join.

"Everyone count your chips," Mr. Donnelly said. "We'll give Simon the average."

James rolled his eyes. "That's going to take awhile."

"And it's too much math," Eve said. "Let's give him what we all started with."

"I'd rather just watch anyway." Simon's mom stood up and motioned to her chair. "Take my place."

Simon moved to comply, but he paused when he noticed her small pile of chips. "What happened here?"

"Oh." She smiled apologetically as she realized she was giving him a poor start. "Drew actually had a good hand."

When Simon appeared sympathetic to the explanation, Drew said, "I don't *always* bluff."

He was first to fold in the next hand to prove his point. Tori won a decent pot on one of his bluffs later on. She finished the game somewhere in the middle. Simon finished only a small stack ahead of her, which meant he'd made up some of his mom's losses. The two of them left together while the others were debating what the next game should be.

"I know what time you're leaving so I know what time to expect a call now," Simon said.

"I might need to give the gentlemen some attention."

"Luckily, you can talk on the phone and pet cats at the same time."

"Lucky for the cats," she said.

Simon smiled at that and squeezed her hand before he let go to head to his car.

Tori got to her house and confirmed that the cats still had food and water. She sat on the couch with her phone where Henry was the first to jump up to join her. She smiled at him while she waited for Simon to answer. It felt like so many other conversations with him, and yet she knew the bond beneath it was deeper. She marveled at how a few words had changed everything and nothing.

20

Though Tori enjoyed her time off for Christmas, she was also looking forward to her first day back at work. They'd be busy, but Ruth and Mr. Sweet would likely find time to share some stories of their Christmas celebrations. She was surprised to see the door to the inner office closed when she entered. Mr. Sweet only closed his door when he thought a client preferred the privacy. It had only happened once in the short time she'd worked there.

The agency didn't officially open for ten more minutes. Had someone come in early?

Then Tori noticed a coat on the back of Ruth's chair. Ruth was talking to Mr. Sweet. It had to be about the baby. Tori was thrilled that Ruth was hopeful enough to start telling everyone. But then she wiped the smile off her face. Was she supposed to pretend she didn't know before Mr. Sweet? The door opened before she had any other thoughts about how to act.

Ruth was smiling. Mr. Sweet was a step behind her. He leaned against his doorframe looking more subtly happy.

"I'm going to have a baby!" Ruth exclaimed.

"Congratulations!" Tori moved to give her a quick hug, a natural reaction regardless of any previous conversations.

Ruth accepted the hug and then smoothed the front of her dress to accentuate a bump. She was showing already?

"When are you due?" Tori asked.

"End of May."

"May!?" Tori did enough math to know Ruth had been quiet for longer than she'd guessed.

"Yes, May." Ruth gestured to Mr. Sweet. "We needed to talk because I don't know if I want to come back after he's born or how much time I want to take if I do and..."

"You already know it's a boy?" Tori frowned at her own interruption.

Ruth nodded and seemed to appreciate the excitement.

Mr. Sweet was also patient about getting Tori caught up.

Ruth continued. "He wants to spend the next few months making sure you're as good as me, then start looking to hire someone who knows the position might be temporary."

"I do," Mr. Sweet said. "And I'm actually glad she waited so long to tell me since now I know I'll still have at least one competent assistant."

Tori was flattered he could say that about her, and mean it, when she was still learning.

"I do have a meeting right after lunch. Let's see how much we can all get done before then," Mr. Sweet pushed himself off the doorway, nodded with satisfaction and turned towards his desk.

Tori took her seat and looked to Ruth for instructions, eager to prove she was competent. The morning disappeared in a flurry of phone calls and reports and spreadsheets, though Ruth still found time to tell Tori about a maternity top Gabe got her for

Christmas. It had ruffles everywhere, and Ruth said it reminded her of the scene in *It's a Wonderful Life* when Clarence says he didn't have time to find stylish underwear. She'd try to wear it at least once for Gabe's sake.

Ruth's brother Isaac had been bragging about winning the tree undecorating. Tori shared some of the highlights from the event, particularly the people who were overly dramatic when hearing their times and the woman who insisted on grouping all the ornaments by color no matter what it did to her time. Tori wanted to tell Ruth that something had changed between her and Simon. There wasn't a natural opening before lunch though.

Tori bundled herself into her coat and burgundy hat with a big pompom to go home to eat. She warmed up a bowl of tomato soup. Something warm sounded good and something vegetably seemed appropriate when she'd been eating more junk food than usual. Henry jumped on the chair next to her and put a paw on the table.

"No." She pushed him back to the chair. The kitchen table was one of the only places her cats weren't allowed. She wouldn't be surprised to find out they jumped on it when she wasn't looking. But if she didn't see it, she could pretend it didn't happen.

He tried again. "No." This time she pushed the chair under the table. She felt Fitz or George walking around her ankles. The cats were nice company, but Tori still wanted to talk to Simon. She had left for lunch a bit late so he was probably home now. There were no lessons Monday afternoons. She pulled out her phone. She was disappointed when she heard his voicemail, not because he was unavailable but because her heart fluttered childishly at the sound of his recorded voice.

"I don't think you'd like tomato." Tori looked down at Fitz. He was sitting by her chair as though he was begging. "You're a carnivore," she reminded him.

He gave a quiet meow. She rewarded him with a quick neck rub, which was what she knew he wanted anyway. Tori put her coat back on as soon as she was finished eating. There was some time left in her break. But if she couldn't talk to Simon, she'd spend it talking with Ruth.

That plan changed as she stepped outside. She froze as she was about to lock the door behind her. Simon was on the gravel about to cut across her yard. He held red and green flowers she assumed were for her, and not from his mom this time. His pace didn't change when he saw her, and she didn't move from her porch. The minute it took for him to meet her by her front door was filled with delightful anticipation.

"Hi," she said. "I just tried to call you."

"Sorry I missed that."

"This is better," she said, glancing at the flowers.

Simon took the opportunity to hand them to her. "Sarah guessed that I was buying them for you, and Cassidy, uh, kind of made a big deal about it. I'm afraid you're going to be fielding a lot of questions on Friday."

Tori smiled. Questions about their relationship were not going to bother her like before. The cold air, however, was bothering her. It made her exposed teeth hurt. "Let's go inside for a minute."

She opened the door and motioned Simon through it. All three cats trotted over to meet them, surprised by her return.

"Hello, gentlemen." Simon's sardonic tone didn't stop Henry from kneading the ground at his feet.

Tori barely acknowledged her pets. "Ruth shared some big news today," she said. "She and Gabriel are expecting."

"Oh, wow. That is big. And wonderful." He sounded sincere, but his reaction was somehow forced.

"She's due in May."

"May? That's... less than nine months."

"They kept it secret for a while."

Simon nodded. He still seemed kind of distracted.

"Is something wrong?"

"No. I hope not."

Tori eyed him warily. "You hope not?"

"That's a bad start." He reached for the flowers she was twirling absently. "Let's pretend I just got here."

She laughed as he took the flowers and put his hand on the door as though he was closing it behind himself. She recognized that what she'd thought was distraction was actually nerves, and now that was rubbing off on her.

Simon held the flowers against his chest while he spoke. "I was going to say that I picked these out because they were the most like the ones Sarah put together to go with the pizzas last week, and you said you liked those." He presented the flowers to her. Again.

"Thank you," she said, realizing she hadn't said that the first time. A second chance was good for both of them.

"When we talked yesterday..." Simon stuffed his hands in his coat pockets as he considered his words. "When we talked yesterday about when we could talk about getting married, I got the impression that you are not opposed to the idea at all, that you were only trying not to agree to anything in the course of a conversation because... This is where I hope I'm not wrong, but I think when you suggested a couple of months or at least several weeks..." He paused to emphasize that those were her words, and she remembered saying exactly that. "I think you were not saying you needed more time, that you only wanted to throw the question forward so I could formally ask you."

That was what she'd meant. She held her breath as she waited to find out if the formal question was next.

Simon seemed encouraged when she didn't correct him. He took a deep breath of his own, and then got down on one knee.

Henry immediately zipped back and forth through the tunnel that created. They both fought amused smiles as they tried to ignore his interference.

"Tori, I feel now that I wasted a lot of time not saying what I wanted to say, and that makes me want to say everything I want to say, which is that I want to marry you. I want to start spending all of my life with you as soon as possible. And so I want to ask you... will you marry me?" He quickly pulled something small out of his pocket.

Tori assumed it was a ring, but she couldn't see very well because of all the water pooling in her eyes. She blinked to release it, then wiped it off her cheeks as she said, "Yes. Yes!"

He took her left hand. "I don't know if this'll even fit. It was my grandma's ring. Grandpa Will got it for her on their tenth anniversary. If you don't like it, I'll get you whatever you want."

It was only slightly loose. There was a tiny row of alternating diamonds and sapphires. "No, it's pretty. I like it. I like that it's from family. Did you tell Grandpa Will you were going to give it to me?"

Simon laughed. "No. Actually, *he* told *me* I was going to give it to you... about three years ago."

Tori could picture it, and it made her laugh, too.

"You were on your way out," Simon said, getting to his feet, "and I got what I came for. I'll walk you to work while we start talking details."

It was probably better that they left before she was in a rush. The walk was short, but they talked a lot faster than they walked so it wasn't quick. They agreed quickly that they couldn't set a date until they talked to someone at the church. Simon volunteered for the task. She liked his eagerness. The wedding would be small and simple. Though Simon expressed some concern that his idea of simple wouldn't line up with hers, she knew they'd end with something that made them both happy. He gave her a quick kiss before they reached the window of Mr. Sweet's office, then turned to go home while she went back to work.

Ruth was still eating. She hadn't brought much, but she was at her desk trying to sort through some mail and listen to an audiobook while she ate. Tori pulled a vase from under the sink and set her pretty flowers on her desk before she took off her coat.

Ruth put her headphones away and nodded at the flowers. "I guess you talked to Simon."

"Yeah." Tori grinned and held up the hand with her new ring.

Ruth let out a shriek she immediately covered as her eyes went guiltily to Mr. Sweet's closed door. She lowered her hand. "I only meant to observe that you now have the flowers he was holding when he poked his head in here to ask what time you left for lunch. Did he seriously just propose to you!?"

Tori nodded enthusiastically.

"And you... you, uh..." Confused laughter was getting in the way of her question. "We just... I mean, I feel like it just happened. We just had a big talk about how you and Simon are great friends and meant to only be friends and... now you're engaged?"

Tori found the disbelief amusing. She nodded again.

"What happened?"

"I don't know."

"How can you not know?" Ruth's skepticism was on par with her amusement.

"Yeah, I guess I know, I mean I don't know how to make it a short answer. Or maybe that I'm still having trouble believing it myself."

"Well, I am not opposed to a long answer," Ruth said.

Tori tried to summarize. "I think Simon's mom might get some of the credit. She started bugging both of us, independently, to take a closer look at our relationship. I ended up admitting to myself that I did want more and was afraid to... definitely a serious case of denial. And then Simon... I guess he could tell I was opening up to the possibility and... then things got a little complicated because he got frustrated about trying not to say something too soon and mentioned getting married in a way I thought he was kidding and overreacted and... then we finally talked about everything."

"And this was..." her question was interrupted by the phone ringing. She huffed an annoyed sigh but managed to sound professional when she answered. She confirmed an appointment time, then turned back to Tori. "You must have had a big talk with Simon just in the last few days."

"Some yesterday and some the day before."

Ruth nodded. "And then he went right to a proposal?" She sounded more excited now than confused.

"Pretty much," Tori said. "It was so sweet. He said he didn't want to waste any more time not saying what he wanted to say."

"Aw."

"Now we should get to work." Tori pointed reluctantly at her screen as she woke it up.

Ruth agreed, also reluctantly. Within a minute, they were engrossed in work. A few minutes after that, Mr. Sweet's door opened. Tori looked up to smile at the new clients as they left. Mr. Sweet walked them to the main door. He did not go all the way back into his office. He paused at the doorway and asked, "Is everything okay out here?" He was fighting a smile, and it seemed likely he had heard Ruth shriek.

Ruth adopted a contrite expression, then she said, "Tori has news today, too."

Mr. Sweet looked at her expectantly.

"Simon and I are getting married."

"Congratulations! Did this happen over Christmas?"

"No. It happened over lunch."

His eyes widened. "In that case, I'm happy to be one of the first to know. No date yet?"

Tori shook her head. "He wants to do it as soon as possible, but I don't know yet when it will be possible."

He tipped his head thoughtfully, processing the information as he glanced back and forth between his two assistants. He might have been wondering how long it would be before Tori had an announcement similar to Ruth's, and also still wondering if Ruth would return to work. He didn't ask any personal questions of course. He only said, "I think I'm going to start thinking about retirement."

~~ The End ~~

Find out about upcoming books, read excerpts with notes from the author, watch various covers take shape, and much more at www.amandahammbooks.com.

www.ingramcontent.com/pod-product-compliance
Lightning Source LLC
LaVergne TN
LVHW041925090826
845145LV00015B/691

* 9 7 8 1 9 4 3 5 9 8 2 5 0 *